MISSING HEATHER AND BAD WEATHER

A FERN GROVE COZY MYSTERY

ABBY REEDE

PEN-N-A-PAD PUBLISHING

A FERN GROVE COZY MYSTERY

BOOK EIGHT

T racy Adams caught sight of the sparkling diamond engagement ring on her left hand and happily fluttered her fingers. She had been engaged to her wonderful fiancé, Warren, for over two weeks now, but sometimes, as the ring caught the light and created a glittering pattern on the surface next to her, she was still taken by surprise. Warren's proposal over the holidays had been unexpected, but she was delighted at the prospect of spending the rest of her life with him.

"Tracy, are you paying attention?"

She looked over to find her Aunt Rose staring at her. "They asked you a question, dear."

She shook her head and came to her senses. She and her Aunt Rose were seated in two folding chairs in the middle of In Season, the flower shop her aunt owned, and she helped operate. They were being interviewed by the local news station for a short segment on styling winter flowers, and she had zoned out as the reporter chatted with Tiffany, the teenage employee who worked part-time at the shop.

"Sorry," she apologized, smiling as she tucked a lock of

hair behind her ears and straightened up in her chair. "What did you say?"

The reporter grinned. "I asked about your big day. That's a lovely ring."

Tracy beamed, her face turning a deep red as she blushed. "Thank you so much," she murmured as she reached over and gently touched the emerald-cut diamond ring. "He picked it out himself."

"Do you have a date set?" the reporter asked kindly. "Are you thinking of a spring or summer wedding?"

Tracy pursed her lips. She and Warren had quarreled about the wedding date; she had always dreamed of an elegant winter wedding, with a long-sleeve dress, sparkly gold bridesmaid dresses, and a reception filled with poinsettias, holiday wreaths, and Christmas colors. Warren did *not* like the thought of a wedding close to the holidays; his birthday was in November, and he thought stuffing a birthday, Thanksgiving, Christmas, New Year's, and a wedding into a two-month period was too much. They had finally compromised and decided on an October wedding; Tracy had not originally been fond of the conventional aesthetics of a fall wedding, but she was warming up to the idea of getting married outside, surrounded by colorful trees and the warm weather of October in the Pacific Northwest.

"October 8th," she informed them. "Only ten more months. We can hardly wait."

"It will fly by," the reporter assured her. "Enjoy it, Tracy. Being engaged is so much fun."

Tiffany let out a loud sigh. "Can we get back to the interview?" she muttered as Tracy blinked.

Aunt Rose shot the girl a look, but then pasted a smile on her face and nodded. "Yes, let's get back to our conversation. You asked about the best flowers for a winter dinner party, yes?"

The reporter nodded. "Yes, I did."

Tracy smiled. "Violets can be lovely for any winter event," she explained. "Winterberries are ideal for the holiday season, but I think Siberian squill, Salix caprea, or Japanese andromeda can be used so nicely throughout winter."

"What would you say to someone who doesn't like dark, heavy colors?" the reporter followed up. "Someone who prefers a light and airy winter palette?"

"Cyclamen," Aunt Rose said instantly. "Without a question. The color is a pale pink, and it is a perfect flower to transition from winter to spring. Add some Winter Aconite and a handful of violets, and you have a gorgeous winter arrangement."

"Lovely," the reporter commented as she glanced down at her notes. "That nearly wraps up my questions. Is there anything else going on around here that you would like to share, ladies?"

Tracy looked at her Aunt, her eyes sparkling. "Should we tell her?"

"Tell me what?"

Aunt Rose's face broke into a huge grin. "I think we should. Tracy, would you like to share the news?"

Tracy sat up primly. "It's an exciting season for our flower shop," she declared. "We've secured a very exciting deal with Next Move, the moving and real estate company in town."

The reporter raised an eyebrow. "What will you be doing with Next Move?"

Aunt Rose's eyes glittered with joy as she explained their new partnership. "We will be creating and styling flower arrangements for their model homes and houses that are being staged and sold," she explained, the excitement radiating from her face. "We will be making custom designs and using them to help prepare gorgeous houses and model homes for viewing."

"How exciting for you," the reporter cooed kindly as Tracy smiled.

"We are certainly thrilled," Tracy added as she tossed her hair behind her shoulder and straightened in her chair. "This will be a once-in-a-lifetime opportunity for my aunt's business. Next Move is a national organization, and we are hoping that if all goes well with our collaboration with the local branch, the partnership could expand."

"We would love to see flowers and designs from In Season used all over the country," Aunt Rose nodded.

"It sounds like you are on the right track," the reporter commented kindly. She motioned at the camera woman, and then rose from her seat. "That's all the footage I need," she told them as she placed her hands on her tiny waist. "Thank you for your time today. This will be such a lovely segment for the morning news tomorrow."

"Thank you for thinking of us," Aunt Rose told her. "We can't wait to watch it."

They waved goodbye as the reporter and the camera woman left, and then Tracy turned to her aunt and squealed. "We're gonna be on TV. Can you believe it?"

"I can't believe they came all the way here just to talk to us," Aunt Rose murmured.

"We *are* kind of a big deal," Tiffany interjected, snapping her gum as she ran a hand through her hair, twisting the ends in a circular motion. "We're ranked as one of the top flower shops in the Pacific Northwest."

"We are?" Aunt Rose asked incredulously. "How do you know that?"

"Google," Tiffany replied matter-of-factly.

Just then, the front door opened, and the three ladies shivered as the cold air filled the room. It was a chilly day; the snow had finally melted, but it was raining like cats and dogs. A short brunette woman with a pinched face marched in.

"Good morning," Aunt Rose called out as the woman blinked at them. "How can we help you?"

The woman's chin quivered. "You sent the wrong thing," she muttered as she approached the counter, pulling out her phone and opening a photo.

"Excuse me?" Tracy asked in confusion. "Who are you?"

The woman placed her phone on the counter so they could see it. It was a photo of a tall flower arrangement sitting on a marble counter. "I'm an assistant decor manager with Next Move," she informed them, crossing her arms over her chest. "You sent this arrangement to one of our open houses on Dearborn Street."

Aunt Rose studied the image. "Oh yes," she recalled, her face brightening. "The dahlias and the baby's breath. This was such a nice combination. Tiffany put it together all by herself."

"My boss didn't want dahlias," the woman complained, her brow furrowing. "She specifically asked for crocus."

Tiffany raised an eyebrow. "For the house at 911 Dearborn Street?" she asked, her face dark.

"Yes, 911 Dearborn Street."

Tiffany scowled. "The order requested dahlias," she insisted. "I remember because of the address; it seemed funny to have someone live at 911, and I remember the caller instructing me to only use the freshest dahlias."

The unhappy woman shook her head. "My boss insists she asked for crocus. She hates dahlias."

"We don't even have crocus right now," Tracy countered. "Tiffany *couldn't* have taken an order for crocus. We haven't had crocus in stock for the last three weeks."

"My boss asked for crocus," the woman declared in a shrill,

nervous voice. "You have to have crocus. Maybe in a freezer or a closet somewhere? If I don't return to the Dearborn Street house with crocus, she says she is going to fire me."

Tiffany's eyes widened. "What? Why? The dahlia arrangement was so pretty. What's her problem?"

Aunt Rose gave the woman a sympathetic look. "It sounds like your boss had a miscommunication of some sort," she told her. "Is there any way we can help? Like Tracy said, we don't have crocus in stock, but we could do a little arrangement of camellias? What about English Primrose?"

The woman's face paled. "She said crocus," she repeated, her voice shaking. "She is going to be so angry with me. She said she will tarnish my reputation if I don't get this right. I'll never get another job."

Tracy stared at her. "Who is your boss?" she asked curiously. "Jason, our contact at Next Move, has always been great."

The woman frowned. "Jason is awesome," she agreed. "But this lady is a dragon; they sent her down from the corporate office in Seattle, and she is so scary. She says she grew up around here, so I hope she doesn't get too comfortable and stay in town forever. We are all ready for her to go back to the city."

Aunt Rose sighed. "What's her name?" she asked. "Maybe I know her and can give her a call to smooth things over? I don't want you to be in trouble, dear."

The woman shook her head. "I don't want to say. I can't afford to get into any more trouble."

"Oh, come on," Aunt Rose gently prodded. "Who is your boss?"

She gulped. "Heather Blackwood."

Aunt Rose wrinkled her nose. "Doesn't sound familiar. Tracy? Do you know her? Heather Blackwood?"

"I don't think I do," she told her Aunt. "I knew a Heather, but her last name was Hampton."

The woman bit the nails on her right hand nervously. "I had better get back," she told them dourly.

"Do you want us to throw together a different arrangement?" Aunt Rose asked in concern. "I'm happy to do it."

"If you don't have crocus, there is no use," the woman muttered as she hung her head and left the shop.

Tracy, Tiffany, and Aunt Rose looked at each other with blank expressions. "That was certainly strange," Aunt Rose finally said. "Heather Blackwood wanted crocus? I've never even heard of her."

"I hope this doesn't affect our partnership with Next Move," Tracy worried as she thought about the terrified expression of the employee.

"We didn't do anything wrong," Tiffany insisted, holding her head high. "The arrangement I made was *beautiful*, and the only emergency at 911 Dearborn Street is the witch who decided she wanted crocus. If I ever meet Heather Blackwood, I'll tell her what I think about her little crocus problem."

"And what do you think?"

Their heads turned sharply as the front door opened and a woman around Tracy's age walked in. She was tall and thin, with a blunt blonde bob that fell just above her shoulders, bright red lipstick, and a designer handbag that Tracy knew cost more than she made in six months at the flower shop.

"Can I help you?" she asked the woman, who was standing before them with her hands on her hips. She wore a monochromatic beige suit with a red scarf tied fashionably around her neck.

"I want to know what that girl would say to Mrs. Blackwood," the woman demanded. "I'm Mrs. Blackwood, and it sounds like we have a little problem, don't we?"

2

T racy's eyes widened as she stared at Mrs. Blackwood. She squinted, and realization washed over her. "Heather? Heather Hampton? Is that you?"

Mrs. Blackwood nodded. "Tracy... *obviously*," she sighed as she set her handbag on the counter and crossed her arms over her bosom. "It's only been twenty years since we graduated high school, not a thousand. We all look more or less the same, don't we? Well, I see I look the same. You look like you've grown up and *out* a bit, dear."

Tracy felt her stomach churn. Heather Blackwood, nee Hampton, had been one of the most popular girls at Fern Grove High School. She had been the head cheerleader, prom queen, the president of the student council, and the lead soloist in the varsity choir. Tracy and Heather had shared several classes together, and while Tracy had been well-liked in school, Heather had never paid her any attention; with her curvy figure and love for mathematics, Tracy had not been cool enough to be in Heather's inner circle, and while they shared some of the same friends, Heather had barely looked Tracy's way in school. They had worked together once on a calculus project, but Heather had bailed on the group meetings, and Tracy ended up completing the project alone.

Now, twenty years later, Tracy could not believe Heather Hampton was standing in front of her. She was dressed elegantly, and Tracy saw an enormous wedding ring on her left hand. "It's nice to see you, Heather," Tracy said politely. "I heard you were back in town."

Heather rolled her eyes. "Not exactly by choice. My company sent me down here to make sure things were running smoothly," she declared. "And clearly, they are not; I've had to fix so many mistakes. It's exhausting. Which, in fact, is why I am here today."

Tracy raised an eyebrow. "Mistakes?"

"The staging is all wrong," Heather announced. "The furniture they've chosen looks cheap, the lighting is unflattering, and the florals your shop has provided just don't quite do it for me."

Tracy folded her arms over her chest. "What do you mean?"

Heather continued, her brows furrowed. "Those dahlias you sent over? No. Just... no. Dahlias aren't appropriate for a luxury home... though you likely wouldn't know that, would you? Crocus is what I asked for, and when I ask for something, I expect to receive it."

Tiffany balled her hands into fists. "I have the receipt," she insisted. "From when your company called the order in. They asked for *dahlias*. I *didn't* mess up the order."

Aunt Rose stepped in. "Of course you didn't, dear," she agreed quietly, patting Tiffany on the shoulder. "Ma'am," she addressed Heather. "Certainly we can work something out. We are so excited about our partnership with your company, and we want you to be satisfied."

Heather blinked. "I don't want anything that looks cheap," she began, her eyes flying to the engagement ring on Tracy's hand. "Though it seems like cheap is a pretty common occurrence around here," she mumbled as she lifted her gaze back to Aunt Rose.

"Excuse me?" Tracy asked, feeling the anger swell in her chest. "What is that supposed to mean?"

"What?" Heather fluttered her eyelashes innocently. "Sorry, I was just talking to myself."

Tiffany glowered at her. "I don't think so," she hissed as she turned and stormed into the back room.

"I want floral arrangements that are elegant and timeless," Heather continued, tossing her hair as she glanced around the flower shop. "Not like what I see in here…"

"Hey!" Tracy interjected, moving to stand in front of her aunt. "That's enough. We don't need your rude, snarky comments. My aunt designs the most beautiful arrangements in the area; that's how we got the partnership with your company in the first place. I think you need to check yourself and show her some respect."

Heather laughed. "Oh Tracy, I remember you were always so quiet in high school," she commented as she lifted her right hand and checked her nails. "What a pity you didn't stay quiet. Look, my company pays a lot of money to stage homes, and I don't think it's out of line to ask for exactly what I want."

"We can make this work," Aunt Rose agreed, nodding as Heather flashed her a bright smile.

"See? That's what I like to hear," Heather lifted her chin haughtily. "I haven't been impressed with your work *yet*, but I'm hoping to give it another chance."

Tracy shook her head. "Wait a second," she insisted as she stepped in front of her aunt. "That's enough. You don't get to come in here, insult my aunt, the owner of this store, and then waltz out like you own the place."

"I mean, I kind of do," Heather laughed sweetly. "My company is giving you a lot of business, enough business to last a few years, I would imagine. So... I kind of *do* own the place."

"You don't," Tracy stated matter-of-factly. "My aunt does. And she does some of the most beautiful work on the West Coast."

Heather sniffed. "Honey, this small town flower shop is cute, but it doesn't compare with the florists in LA, Seattle, or Portland."

Tracy's face flushed with rage. "I think you should leave," she warned Heather as she felt the anger rising in her chest. "Now."

Heather shrugged. "I'm not sure I'm ready to leave."

"You should go," Tracy repeated, her jaw clenched. "Go and die, for all I care..."

Heather's eyes widened. "Excuse me? What did you just say to me?"

Tracy's heart pounded. "Nothing. I just said you should leave."

"You *threatened* me," Heather accused Tracy, pointing a finger at her chest. "You threatened to kill me."

Aunt Rose stepped in. "I don't think she meant any harm," she assured Heather. "Tracy is just... tired today. Tracy, why don't you run to the back room for a bit."

Heather did not lower her finger, which was still directed at Tracy. "She threatened me," she repeated, shaking her head. "I should call the cops."

"Please don't do that," Aunt Rose begged. "Tracy was just joking. She can be such a silly woman."

Heather narrowed her eyes. "I hope you're right," she hissed as she glared at Tracy. "My company won't like to hear about this. I'm not sure we can do business with people who *threaten* us."

Aunt Rose clasped her hands together. "Please," she pleaded with Heather. "Tracy was kidding. She didn't mean any harm. Right, Tracy?"

Tracy saw the look of desperation on her aunt's face, and she realized that she had possibly put the business deal with Next Move in jeopardy. She forced herself to smile and then nodded. "It was just a joke, Heather. My bad. I would never, ever want anything bad to happen to you."

"Good."

Heather turned on her heel. "Have a crocus arrangement at the Dearborn Street house in forty-five minutes or the partnership is over."

She slammed the front door on the way out. Tracy bit her lip as Aunt Rose shook her head. "That was crazy."

Aunt Rose frowned. "You didn't really help things, Tracy. We could have lost that business. Why did you have to run your mouth?"

Tracy's mouth dropped open. "Did you hear the way she spoke to us? She acted like we were trash."

Aunt Rose crossed her arms. "The customer is *always* right, Tracy, and in this case, she was the customer. We can't let our egos get in the way of business. I don't care what kind of a brat she acted like in high school; you need to get over yourself and watch your attitude if you want to continue working at In Season."

Tracy's face darkened. "Are you serious?"

"As a heart attack," Aunt Rose said firmly. "When others act poorly, that doesn't give us permission to. You know that."

Tracy felt tears in her eyes, but she blinked them away. "I think I'm going to go home early," she told her aunt as she removed her apron. "I'm not feeling great right now."

That evening, Warren and Tracy sat together at Beijing Beef, the local Chinese restaurant. Tracy had told Warren about her rotten day, and he had insisted on taking her to dinner. She had not wanted to go, but now, as they sat across from each other holding hands, she felt more relaxed than she had been all day.

"I'm thinking about the crab rangoon," Warren began as he studied his menu. "They have the lobster and cream cheese filling. What do you think?"

She grinned. "That's exactly what I wanted. Can we get the vegetable lo mein and the spring rolls, too?"

"That's my girl," he smiled. "Tell me more about your day. It sounds like you need a drink more than you need Chinese food, my love."

She rolled her eyes. "I just can't believe another adult spoke to me the way Heather Hampton—I mean, Heather *Blackwood* did," she frowned. "No one has *ever* spoken to me that way. And I hated how my aunt tried to grovel instead of stand up for herself."

"That sounds frustrating," Warren agreed, nodding as he gave her hand a squeeze. "I'm so sorry that happened."

She pulled her hand away and perched her head on her hands. "I'm just annoyed," she expressed as the waitress came over to their table. "Heather was rude in high school, and she's rude now. It isn't fair that people get to act in whatever way they choose without consequences."

The waitress fluttered her eyelashes and produced a notepad from her pocket. "May I take your order?"

"We'll start with the crab rangoon, an order of spring rolls, and some vegetable lo mein," Warren told her as he handed her their menus. "Please and thank you."

"No problem," the waitress told them. "Our kitchen is a little backed up right now, so it might be a ten or fifteen minute wait, but I can leave some treats for you."

She reached into her pocket and set two fortune cookies on the table. "I'll go put that order in."

The waitress scurried away. Tracy picked up a fortune cookie and placed it in front of her fiancé. "Open it!"

He shook his head. "I don't believe in this sort of stuff," he protested, but she opened the wrapper and placed it in his hands.

"Come on, babe," she insisted. "Live a little. At least read your fortune. I want to hear it."

Warren cracked open the cookie and pulled out the thin sliver of paper. He set the cookie aside and turned his gaze to his fortune. "You will have a long, happy life," he read. "That's boring. I bet every fortune says something like that."

She shook her head. "Warren," she said in annoyance. "Don't ruin it for me. I think fortune cookies are fun."

Tracy took the other cookie and opened the wrapper, tearing the cookie open and finding the fortune. "I wonder what it says," she giggled gleefully as she held the paper between her thumbs and index fingers.

Her face fell. "That isn't fun."

Warren reached over to take the slip, but she stuffed it into her pocket. "What did it say?" her fiancé asked. "I want to read yours."

"Just forget about it."

Warren shot her a look. "Tracy…"

"Fine," she replied as she pulled the crumpled paper out of her pocket. "Darkness will soon befall you and bad luck will fall on your life like a heavy rainstorm. Be careful."

Warren laughed. "Honey, why are you so upset? It's just a fake fortune. These things aren't real."

She bit her lip. "I think it's real."

He sighed. "We'll just switch, babe. I'll take the darkness, and you can have the good fortune. Deal?"

"I don't think it works like that."

Suddenly, Warren's radio started buzzing; he worked as a police officer, and that evening, he happened to be on call. "Sorry," he mouthed apologetically as he turned down the volume on the radio. "I can call them back."

"It's okay," she told him. "Just take the call."

Warren fiddled with the receiver and pressed it to his ear. His face paled. "Oh goodness," he muttered as he rose from his seat.

"What is it?"

His eyes filled with worry. "Missing person report," he told her. "I think I need to go. I'm so sorry, Tracy…"

"Wait," she stopped him. "Who is missing? Is it someone in town?"

He shook his head. "I'll tell you later, babe. I have to go."

"Warren?"

He turned around and hung his head. "It's Heather Black-wood," he muttered. "Heather Blackwood has gone missing."

3

O ne week later, Tracy, Tiffany, and Aunt Rose were leaning against the counter at the flower shop with three coffees sitting in front of them. It was a dark, rainy morning, which was fitting given Tracy's horrible mood.

"Calluna vulgaris," Aunt Rose chatted to Tiffany as Tracy's mind wandered. "Not heather."

"Heather?" Tracy snapped back to attention. "What about her? Has she been found?"

Tiffany shook her head. "We were talking about the flower, Tracy," she informed her. "But Heather Blackwood? I heard she ran off to Mexico with a secret boyfriend," Tiffany whispered as she reached below the counter and held up the local newspaper, which bore a black-and-white photo of Heather Blackwood on the front page.

While the Fern Grove police had conducted dozens of searches, sent dogs into the nearby forests, and even sent divers into the Pacific Ocean, no trace of Heather Blackwood had been found. Warren hadn't had much to say about her disappearance; he was busy working on the case, and Tracy had barely seen him since their dinner at Beijing Beef. He *did* mention, however, that Heather Blackwood was nowhere to be found, and as she thought about the strange disappearance of her old classmate, Tracy was filled with a deep sense of dread.

"A secret boyfriend?" Aunt Rose scowled. "Tiffany, that is unkind; the woman is missing, and it is not nice of you to make up stories about it."

"That's what people are saying," she insisted defensively. "I'm just repeating what I heard."

Aunt Rose furrowed her brow. "Mrs. Blackwood is a married woman, Tiffany. It's inappropriate to start rumors about her having a secret boyfriend."

"She had plenty of secret boyfriends in high school," Tracy added casually as Tiffany's jaw dropped. "She was always dating two or three guys at once."

"See?" Tiffany cried, turning to face Aunt Rose. "I knew it."

Aunt Rose shot Tracy a look. "Don't encourage her," she warned. "Not everyone behaves well in high school, and it is certainly ungenerous to hold old grudges twenty years later, dear. I can think of a few times when *you* were out of line as a teenager, and I'm sure you wouldn't want me to mention those instances, would you?"

Tiffany's eyes widened. "You have dirt on Tracy?" she squealed in delight. "Spill, Aunt Rose. I want to hear all the bad stories about her."

Tracy scowled. "*Enough*," she muttered as she adjusted her ponytail. "I don't want to talk about Heather anymore."

"Heather? Or heather?" Tiffany teased.

"Both," Tracy sighed.

Aunt Rose turned to glance at Tiffany. "Let's get back to

talking about the arrangements for Next Move," she suggested. "Did you use heather for the crocus arrangement?"

"Person Heather? Or Plant heather?" Tiffany teased.

"*Tiffany…*" Aunt Rose warned.

"Sorry," she groaned.

Aunt Rose pasted a smile on her face. "Let's change the subject, shall we? Did I tell you girls I got a new cell phone?"

She pulled a rose gold iPhone out of her pocket and held it up proudly for them to see. "What do you think?"

"I love it," Tiffany shrieked as she reached for the device. "It's such a pretty color."

Aunt Rose winked at Tracy. "Thank goodness we have Tiffany," she commented as Tiffany started tapping the phone's shiny screen. "I don't have any idea how to use a smartphone. I need her to give me a lesson or two."

"Is this the latest iPhone?" Tiffany asked as she studied the phone's built-in camera.

"It is," Aunt Rose said proudly.

Tiffany grinned. "This has one of the best cellphone cameras around," she praised as she lifted the phone up and posed for the camera. "Let's take a selfie."

"A selfie?"

Tiffany lowered the phone and stared at her. "You don't know what a selfie is?"

Aunt Rose shook her head. "What is it? How do we take it?"

Tiffany giggled. "You stand here," she instructed as she positioned Aunt Rose in front of a display of winter jasmine. "This is a perfect background for a group photo. Tracy?"

"I don't want to be in the photo," Tracy grumbled, and Tiffany moved to stand by her aunt.

"A selfie is a self-portrait." She explained to Rose. "Taking a selfie means taking a self-portrait. Let's snap one!"

Tiffany flashed a dazzling smile, and Aunt Rose copied her, turning her lips upward and batting her eyelashes. "One... two... three."

They took the photo and immediately turned the phone around to examine it. "It's gorgeous," Tiffany cried. "You should make this your Facebook profile picture."

Aunt Rose laughed. "I think I'm a little late to the party on this one," she admitted sheepishly. "But what is a face book?"

Tiffany's jaw dropped. "You don't know what Facebook is?"

Aunt Rose shook her head, and Tiffany took her hand. "I have a lot to show you," she murmured as she gave Rose's hand a squeeze. "Aunt Rose, I'm about to change your life."

Later that evening, Tracy left the flower shop and headed home. It was pouring rain, and as she dashed through the streets, she felt her hair and clothes getting wet. Tracy shivered; it was a heavy, punishing rain, and the drops hurt as they smacked her skin.

Her stomach rumbled, and she put her hand on her belly. She was hungry and ready to make dinner, but realized she hadn't done any grocery shopping for the week. She thought about ordering in, but shook her head, remembering that she was planning and budgeting for a wedding, and she probably should eat at home. She decided to make her own dinner, and she popped into the grocery store to grab some ramen.

"Hey, dear," Kim, the owner, called out to her as she walked inside. "I haven't seen you in a minute! Come over here and say hello."

Tracy stifled a groan; Kim had a larger-than-life personality and could talk someone's ear off, and she just wasn't in the mood to deal with Kim's antics. She tried to wave Kim off, but the store owner dashed over to her and gave her a big hug.

"I haven't seen you since the big news," Kim squealed as she pawed at Tracy's left hand. "Show me the ice, baby."

Tracy reluctantly held up her hand and gave her fingers a little waggle. "That ring is stunning," Kim complimented as she peered at the diamond. "I heard he proposed at the gazebo? How romantic."

"Thanks," Tracy smiled weakly. "We're very excited."

Kim pulled back and studied Tracy. "You're drenched," she laughed as she surveyed Tracy's jacket, which was hanging limply on her shoulders. "Need a towel?"

"That's okay."

Kim raised an eyebrow. "Are you sure? You look a little upset. What's going on, Tracy?"

Tracy felt the weight of the last week collapse on her, and she stifled tears. "There's just a lot going on," she explained as she clutched the box of ramen to her chest. "I'm really stressed out."

"Clearly," Kim agreed. "Why are you so stressed? You're newly engaged. You should be walking on sunshine."

Tracy wrinkled her nose. "I think I've been cursed," she said in a hushed voice.

"Cursed? How?" Kim asked, her eyes wide with wonder.

Tracy bit her lip. "Are you superstitious? Do you believe in things like magic, ghosts, or luck?"

Kim nodded. "I *am* superstitious. Everyone in my family is," she confirmed.

"I was eating at Beijing Beef the other night," Tracy began. "And I got a fortune cookie. It told me I was going to have a streak of bad luck. Ever since that happened, I've been feeling really anxious and down, and I'm worried that something bad is about to happen."

Kim's face paled. "You received a sign," she muttered as she nervously ran a hand through her black hair. "A very clear sign…"

"A sign?"

Kim stared into her face. "You need to be careful, Tracy," she whispered as Tracy's heart pounded. "It sounds like bad luck is going to befall you, and I don't think there is anything you can do to stop it."

4

"And now, I have two thousand friends! Can you believe it?"

The next morning, Tracy, Aunt Rose, and Tiffany were gathered around a table at Roast, a new coffee shop in town. Aunt Rose was showing them her cell phone, eagerly filling them in on her new social media accounts.

"Facebook is so fun," she chirped as she flipped through some photos she had uploaded of herself. "I connected with some friends from elementary school. Can you believe that? I grew up in Indiana and didn't move here until middle school, and I've found friends I thought I would never see again."

Tiffany grinned. "That's the best part of social media," she told Rose as she twirled her spoon in her latte. "My mom was adopted, and she found her birth mother on Facebook. They were able to meet in person, and now, I have an extra grandmother. It's so cool."

Aunt Rose batted her eyelashes. "I wonder if I could find someone special using social media," she wondered aloud. "I put a bunch of cute photos of myself on my profile. Maybe I should take a few more?"

Tracy bit her lip. "I don't think that's the best idea," she cautioned her aunt. "Social media can be great, but it can be dangerous. People can steal your photos and information. It happens all the time."

"Don't be silly," Tiffany scolded her. "Tracy, that sounds paranoid. Facebook is a place where people can meet and connect. I met one of my favorite boyfriends on Facebook, in fact. Abdullah and I aren't together anymore, but I loved chatting with him online and sending pictures back and forth."

"Abdullah?" Aunt Rose asked. "That's a fancy name."

"He was a Saudi prince," Tiffany said dreamily. "He was so handsome. He wanted me to come live with him in the middle east, but my parents said no."

Tracy frowned. "How do you know he was a prince?"

"He told me so," Tiffany replied defensively. "He told me he was a prince. He sent me photos of his palace and the jewels he wanted to give me."

Tracy gave Aunt Rose a look. "See? Some guy online tricked Tiffany into believing he was a prince. What if she had bought a ticket to go to Saudi Arabia? It could have been anyone on the other end of the internet. There is just no safe way to know, Aunt Rose."

Tiffany glowered at her. "I think you're just jealous," she said, sticking her nose up in the air. "You've never had the attention of a prince, and you're jealous of me."

Tracy laughed out loud. "Yeah, right, you caught me," she sighed sarcastically. "I'm so jealous of your Persian prince, Tiffany."

"He was a *Saudi* prince," Tiffany cried.

Tracy felt her cell phone buzz in her pocket, and she opened it to see a call from an unknown number. "Hello?"

"Tracy?"

"This is she."

"This is Next Move calling," a female voice told her. "How are you today?"

"I'm well. What can I do for you?" Tracy asked.

"We need to place an urgent order," the woman explained. "There's been a last-minute showing of a house on Marshall Street scheduled for this afternoon, and the sellers have requested some staging. We need a few floral arrangements for the kitchen and bathrooms sent over immediately. Is that possible?"

"Of course," Tracy assured her. "You said the house is on Marshall Street?"

"111 Marshall Street," the caller confirmed. "We need a large arrangement and two small arrangements. It really doesn't matter what plants you use; the sellers' home decor is mostly neutral, so anything will go."

"Okay," Tracy told her. "No problem at all. We will get something put together and deliver it as soon as we can."

"Wonderful," the woman said. "Just email us an invoice and we will get the bill taken care of. Thank you so much."

Tracy hung up the phone and turned to her Aunt and Tiffany. "We need to get to In Season," she informed them. "We have an urgent order that just came in."

"An urgent order? From whom?" Aunt Rose asked.

"Next Move."

Aunt Rose shook her head. "No," she shook her head firmly. "I don't think it's a good idea. Not after what happened with that Blackwood woman. I think we should stay away from Next Move for a while, don't you, Tracy?"

Tracy pursed her lips. "It isn't Next Move's fault that Heather was so rude," she pushed back. "Things were fine with our partnership before Heather, and now, she's gone. I think it would be fine to do this order."

Aunt Rose turned to Tiffany. "What do you think?"

Tiffany shrugged. "I think it's fine," she told her. "Heather didn't hurt my feelings. She was rude and nasty, and that reflects on *her*, not me."

Aunt Rose nodded. "If you're sure," she told them. "Let's get moving; if we get back to the shop in the next fifteen minutes, we can throw together some gorgeous cyclamen and eucalyptus; those would look so nice for a showing."

An hour later, Tracy was standing on the porch of 111 Marshall Street. It was a stunning brick home with intricate landscaping and tall windows. The porch featured an assortment of expensive looking outdoor furniture, and the massive front door was painted red.

Tracy rang the doorbell and waited patiently, balancing two large plastic bags filled with the floral arrangements. Tiffany had put together three lovely pieces, and as Tracy glanced at the house, she imagined they would look perfect inside.

No one came to the door, and Tracy rang the bell again. "Hello?" She gave the front door a hard knock, but no one appeared. She checked her watch; it had been over an hour since she had received the call from Next Move, and she needed to get the plants inside.

Tracy jiggled the handle of the front door and was pleasantly surprised to find the house was unlocked. She cautiously stepped inside. "Hello? Is anyone here? It's Tracy from In Season. I have a plant delivery for you."

No one answered her, and she carefully removed her shoes, not wanting to track in dirt or mud onto the pristine white carpets. She set the plants down beside her and pulled out her cell phone, dialing Aunt Rose's number.

"Honey?" her aunt answered on the second ring. "What's up, dear? Did the delivery go okay?"

Tracy raised an eyebrow. "That's the problem," she murmured as she slowly backed out of the house and closed the door behind her. "There is no one here. I wanted to make sure I had the right address."

"111 Marshall Street," Aunt Rose told her. "Right?"

"That's where I am," Tracy glanced up at the numbers on the door. "But no one is home. It's deathly quiet. Usually the real estate agent or the sellers are at the house to greet us."

"Hmmm," Aunt Rose replied. "That is odd. Did you call Next Move?"

Tracy smiled softly. "That's my next move," she joked. "I'll talk to you later."

She hung up the call, but before she could dial Next Move, she heard the wail of sirens. She glanced around and saw two police cars racing down the street toward her. They swung into the driveway and parked, and five officers descended upon the house.

"Freeze," a tall female officer ordered her as she dropped the plants and held up her hands. "Step away from the house and lay down on the ground."

"What's going on?" Tracy cried as she obeyed her orders, throwing herself on the ground as an officer stood over her with a gun. "I'm just delivering flowers."

"Quiet down," the officer warned. Tracy watched as the other three officers ran into the house, their guns drawn.

There was some static on the female officer's radio, and Tracy heard a voice. "Missing person has been found," one of the officers informed them over the radio. "Heather Blackwood has been found."

Tracy shuddered. What was going on? Why was Heather Blackwood hiding out in the house on Marshall Street?

"Alive or dead?" the officer standing beside her asked.

There was a long pause. The radio buzzed, and Tracy's stomach dropped as the officer replied. "Dead," he told them. "Heather Blackwood is dead."

5

As she lay against the cold, wet ground, Tracy wanted to throw up; Heather Blackwood was *dead*? She felt confused and worried. Why had she received a call to deliver flowers to a house where Heather Blackwood's dead body was waiting to be discovered? Why was Heather Blackwood *in* the house at 111 Marshall Street? These questions raced through Tracy's mind, and she bit her lip to keep from crying as the coroner showed up in her van fifteen minutes later.

"What's going on?" she asked the officer whose gun was still pointed directly at her back. "Can I get up now?"

The officer turned to greet the coroner who was holding a black leather bag. They spoke for a few moments, and then another officer came over to escort the coroner inside of the house.

"Can I call my fiancé?" Tracy whispered. "Please?"

The officer shook her head. "Ma'am, you will be granted your call when we arrive at the police station. For now, I would advise you stop talking."

"Why? What is going on?"

The officer bent down and took Tracy's hand, helping her to her feet. The shrill cry of an ambulance grew louder, and a moment later, it pulled into the driveway behind the two police cars. Four paramedics emerged from the back, lowering a metal gurney from the bay and carefully rolling it into the house.

"Can I please call my fiancé now?" Tracy asked again. "I want to talk with him."

The officer spun her around and snapped a pair of shiny silver handcuffs on Tracy's wrists. "You have the right to remain silent. Anything you say can and will be used against you in a court of law. You have the right to an attorney. If you cannot afford an attorney, one will be provided for you. Do you understand the rights I have just read to you? With these rights in mind, do you wish to speak to me?"

"I'm under arrest?" Tracy questioned, her eyes growing huge as she realized what was happening. "Why?"

The officer stared at her. "Ma'am, I would strongly suggest you save your questions and comments until we get to the station and your attorney is present."

"But I didn't do anything," Tracy insisted as she squirmed in the handcuffs. "And these are too tight. They hurt. Please let me go. This is all a misunderstanding."

"That's what they all say," the officer muttered under her breath as she helped Tracy into the backseat of the police car.

An hour later, Tracy was led into the police station. Her face was tear-stained, and her voice was raw from crying. As they rounded a corner, she breathed a sigh of relief as a familiar face came into view. Warren rushed toward her, a frantic expression in his eyes. "What is going on?" he whispered as he embraced her.

"Warren, back off," the female officer warned. "She's heading into questioning."

Warren stood his ground. "This is my future wife," he declared as he wrapped an arm around Tracy's shoulder. "Give us a minute."

"I'm not allowed to do that."

Warren shot her a desperate look. "Please," he pleaded quietly, his face crumbling as he begged the officer. "Please let me talk to her. Just for a minute. I'll be quick and discrete. Please? I love this woman, and she needs me."

The woman narrowed her eyes, but she stepped away from Tracy. "One minute," she warned as she turned her back on them.

Warren kissed Tracy on the forehead and then pulled back to look into her eyes. "What is going on?"

She quickly told him the story of how she had been having coffee with her Aunt and Tiffany, but their chat had been interrupted by a call from Next Move. "I rushed over with the delivery, but no one was home. I thought it was weird, and I called Aunt Rose to double check the address," she explained as Warren nodded. "Before I knew it, the police were rolling Heather's dead body out of the house."

Warren took a deep breath. "I know you had nothing to do with any of this mess," he assured her as he took her by the shoulders. "I think it'd be great to have a lawyer go with you into the interview."

"A lawyer? But you just said you knew I had nothing to do with it," she said, rubbing her sweaty palms on her sides.

"I just feel funny about you going in there all by yourself."

"There's nothing to feel funny about. I know I didn't do anything wrong."

"Time's up," the officer told them as she came back and put her hand on Tracy's shoulder. "They are doing some questioning in the second interview room down the main hall," she told Warren. "She'll be done around two."

"Thank you," he told her. "I love you, Tracy. Good luck. Just tell the truth and it will all be okay."

Tracy was led into a small room with dim lighting. Two wooden chairs sat facing each other, and she settled into the chair farther from the door. A thin, blonde officer walked in behind her and took the other chair. "Tracy Adams?"

She nodded. "That's me."

"Date of birth? Social security number? Address?"

Tracy rattled off her information. She felt her stomach twist and turn as the officer stared at her; they appeared to be the same age, and she felt intimidated by how serious her chiseled face was.

"How did you know Heather Blackwood?"

Tracy took a deep breath. "We knew each other from high school," she answered.

"What was your opinion of her?"

"Heather had a lot of personality," Tracy replied diplomatically.

"Would you say you were friends?" asked the officer.

"Not friends," Tracy sighed.

"Enemies?"

She felt her body grow cold. "No, not enemies. We didn't interact often in high school or after graduation. In fact, when she walked into my aunt's shop last week, it was the first time I had seen her since our ten year reunion in 2011."

"And what was your interaction with her at your aunt's shop?"

Tracy cleared her throat as she recounted Heather's visit. "Heather was displeased with our shop," she answered honestly. "She didn't approve of the flowers we had sent over, and it was clear she had strong feelings about our work."

"Can you elaborate?"

"She was mean and nasty," Tracy told her. "She had a lot

of rude things to say, and I didn't appreciate the way she was patronizing us."

The officer narrowed her dark brown eyes. "So, you and Heather had an unpleasant encounter?"

"Yes," Tracy agreed. "But it was handled, and we were taking measures to improve our business relationship with her. We weren't able to mend things completely because she went missing, and then…"

The officer looked down at her notes. "Do you dislike Heather Blackwood?"

"Yes. I mean, no. I mean… is that a fair question?"

"So that's a yes?" The officer confirmed. "You dislike Heather Blackwood?"

"No, I mean… yes. No?"

"Let's move on. Did you know Heather Blackwood's body was at 111 Marshall Street?"

"No."

"No? Are you sure?"

"Yes."

"So that's a yes? You knew?" the officer pressed her.

"NO." Tracy replied, though she felt puzzled as she tried to keep up with the questions.

The officer raised an eyebrow. "You seem to be changing your story a lot," she commented as she looked down at her notes. "So, which is it? Yes? No? Are you lying about anything, Ms. Adams?"

Tracy sighed in exasperation. "Yes," she told her, and then her face paled. "I meant no. Sorry, these yes and no questions are confusing me."

The officer's eyes widened. "Why were you at 111 Marshall Street today?"

Tracy repeated what she had told Warren. "I didn't know Heather was there," she breathed as the officer took notes. "I had no idea…"

The officer finished her questions and undid the handcuffs.

"Am I free to go?" Tracy asked, gripping her raw wrists.

"Yes, but your release is conditional," the officer advised her. "You are not under arrest at this moment, but we have reason to believe you were somehow involved in the murder of Heather Blackwood. Let us know if you consider leaving the area."

Her jaw fell open. "You think I did it? I'm a *suspect?*" she asked incredulously.

"I am not at liberty to discuss further details with you," the officer disclosed. "But I strongly recommend you keep your head low and let us know if you want to leave the state."

Tracy felt shellshocked; how had a simple flower delivery escalated into such a mess?

The officer led Tracy out into the main hallway. "Can you please follow me to sign our register to show your time of exit from our premises."

Tracy nodded, and did as she was told. She glanced around; Warren was nowhere in sight. She wondered if he was in his office.

She turned to go and find her fiancé and noticed an older gentleman staring at her. "Can I help you?" she asked with a smile, but the man quickly lowered his gaze.

Her face fell. She could not blame him for staring at her; she was involved in a murder case, and despite knowing she had nothing to do with it, she had no way to prove to the people of Fern Grove that she was *innocent.*

———————————————————

6

After a fruitless search for her fiancé, Tracy left the police station and headed to In Season. She was desperate for a hug, and as she walked into the shop, she ran straight into the arms of her aunt.

"Tracy?" Aunt Rose asked as Tracy's body began to shake in her arms. "What's going on? I tried to call you. Where have you been?"

"They took me to jail," she explained as horror filled her aunt's face.

"Who? Who took you to jail?"

Tracy told her what had happened at the house on Marshall Street. "So Heather Blackwood is dead?" Aunt Rose asked. "Why would Next Move send you over there with flowers? I don't understand what is going on."

"I don't either," Tracy agreed. "I showed up with the flowers and no one was home, and the next thing I knew, I was being questioned at the police station. They think I was involved."

Her aunt's eyes grew huge with concern. "You're a suspect?" she cried. "In a murder?"

"They wouldn't say for sure," Tracy sighed. "But I think I am. I think I'm in big trouble, Aunt Rose."

Tiffany raised her eyebrows, her face drawn. "We know *you* didn't kill Heather," she reassured Tracy. "Let's be honest, Tracy... you can be sassy sometimes, but you couldn't kill a fly."

"But who did?" Tracy wondered as they huddled together. "Who killed her, and why was she in that house?"

She nearly jumped out of her skin as the front door opened and a short brunette woman with a thick waist and large bosom waddled in. "How can we help you?" Aunt Rose asked, forcing herself to smile at the customer.

The woman smiled back, but then her eyes widened as she spotted Tracy. "Oh my gosh," she fretted aloud as she took a step back from the counter.

"Are you okay?" Tiffany asked.

"*She's* here," the woman pointed at Tracy. "Shouldn't she be sitting in a jail cell?"

Aunt Rose frowned. "That is my niece you are talking about," she countered. "And she works here."

The woman's face became pinched. "They let murderers out of jail to work at their normal jobs?" she asked. "I wouldn't trust her around flower tools, if this were my shop. I bet she killed Heather Blackwood with a pair of stem cutters."

"Hey," Tiffany stopped her, moving to stand in front of the woman. "That's enough."

The woman shot her a look and then turned on her heel to leave the shop.

"What was that all about?" Tracy moaned. "People really think I killed her? This is a mess, guys. A big, awful mess."

The front door opened again, and a different woman walked in. She was petite and pale, with straight red hair and a smattering of freckles across her nose. "Hello," she greeted them, but her face fell when she spotted Tracy. "Oh, excuse me…"

"Wait!" Tracy cried out. "Don't leave. I did not kill Heather Blackwood. I didn't have anything to do with it. *Please.*"

The woman stopped. "That rumor *has* been going around town," she told Tracy softly. "But I can hear in your voice that you are telling the truth."

"Really?" Tracy cried out in relief. "Thank you so much."

The woman smiled gently. "Don't worry about it too much," she advised Tracy. "I don't know if you remember me, but I was a few years younger than you in high school. Cally Gill? Anyway, I was on the debate team with Heather, and she was something of a monster. It doesn't surprise me she has some enemies around; she was always an uppity snob. You just take care of yourself and don't let this bring you down."

"Thank you so much," Tracy murmured. "I will try to not let this get to me…."

Cally purchased a small bouquet of lilies and left Tracy staring after her as she went.

"See? Not everyone in town thinks you're a murderer," Tiffany said cheerfully.

Tracy shot her a look. "Gee, thanks," she muttered, taking off her apron. "I'm going to go for a quick walk around the block," she told them. "I need to clear my head…"

She left the shop, her head hung low, feeling miserable as she rounded the corner and turned onto the next street. She could not believe what was happening; how had her average day turned into such a nightmare?

As she walked along the muddy streets, she ran into Pastor Butler, the local minister. "Tracy Adams," he greeted her kindly, his thick mustache curled upward from the humidity. "How are you doing, dear Tracy? I hear you have had quite a day…"

Her face fell. "I'm not a murderer," she mumbled as she looked down at her boots. "I didn't have anything to do with Heather Blackwood's death, Pastor. You *have* to believe me."

Pastor Butler nodded at her, giving her a kind smile. "Tracy, calm down," he urged her.

"I can't calm down," she cried. "Everyone in town thinks I killed Heather Blackwood, and I had nothing to do with it. I went over to that house with some flowers, and then the police showed up. That doesn't mean I killed her."

Pastor Butler put a hand on her shoulder. "Tracy," he murmured. "Please calm down. I *believe* you, my dear. I've known you and your Aunt for years. I know you would never hurt anyone."

Tracy looked up at him, a deep sense of relief filling her belly. "Really?"

He nodded. "Murder is not something to be joked about or to be taken lightly," he said sternly. "And I am sorry people have been accusing you before the facts have come to light."

She gave him a weak smile. "Thank you."

"Of course. Besides, it's not my place to judge; the Lord will pass judgement on whoever did this. It's not my right to cast doubt or judge someone. Poor Heather. Just think, Tracy; dear Heather has already stood before the Lord on her judgement day. Can you imagine? Death is a tragedy, but it gives me great comfort to imagine those who have passed standing before the Lord."

She wrinkled her nose. "I wonder how judgement day went for Heather," she thought to herself, but then shook her head. She shouldn't be thinking rude things about the dead. "Did you know Heather well?" she asked the minister. "She and I went to high school together, but we didn't really keep in touch after."

He nodded. "Heather's family has attended my church for years," he explained. "I imagine they will ask me to officiate her funeral; the Hamptons are wonderful people, and her father has been a pillar of our town. He donated the money for the renovations to the YMCA, the youth center, and the homeless shelter."

"He sounds like quite a guy," Tracy added cautiously, careful not to give away how she felt about Heather. "And her mom? I kind of remember her from events in high school. She was always the head of the PTA and the Prom Committee."

"Mrs. Hampton is an angel on Earth," the Pastor smiled. "She volunteers in the nursery at our church every single week. She also bakes goods for the homeless ministry our church runs."

"What a gem," Tracy sighed. "Heather's parents sure sound lovely."

"They are," he agreed. "Heather was always a little different; she had a strong personality and fiery spirit, but her heart was in the right place; when she was a girl, she used to donate her allowance to the offering at Church every week, and she kept up her charitable donations even when she grew up and moved to the city."

"I didn't know that," Tracy whispered.

"Heather wasn't always the sweetest," he told her. "But she meant well. It's a tragedy that she's left us so soon..."

Tracy bit her lip. "I just wish we knew what happened."

He peered at her curiously. "I heard it happened at a house on Marshall Street. 111 Marshall Street?? Do you know who lives there, Tracy?"

She shook her head. "I don't," she told him. "But mark my words, I'm going to find out."

7

After saying goodbye to Pastor Butler, Tracy felt much better as she wandered back to In Season. *Someone* in town believed she was innocent and she was hopeful as she neared the flower shop. Perhaps everything would all blow over, and if she continued telling the truth, it would all work out okay.

As she approached the front door, she was nearly blinded by the light of a camera flashing in her face. "Tracy Adams? Tracy Adams, do you have a moment to talk?"

She blinked, her eyes feeling raw from the bright lights. "Excuse me?"

Her watery eyes opened, and she gasped as she saw Burt Brock, an anchor from a national television news show, standing in front of her. He was dressed in a corduroy suit and holding a microphone in his hand. A few paces away, two men with cameras perched on their shoulders were watching them, and Burt gave them a signal.

"It's her," he called over to them. "It's Tracy Adams."

Tracy stared at Burt. He was much shorter than he

appeared to be on television, and she could see gray hairs growing along his temples. "Can I help you?"

Burt flashed her a bright smile. "Tracy, what do you have to say about the murder of Heather Blackwood, executive at Next Move?"

Tracy's face paled. "What?"

He stuck the microphone in her face. "Heather Blackwood," he repeated. "What do you have to say about her murder?"

She felt sick. The cameras were pointing directly at her face, and she knew she looked nervous. "No comment," she said quietly as she tried to move inside the flower shop.

Burt moved to block her entrance. "Just a few words?" he prodded, and Aunt Rose appeared, shoving past Burt and moving to stand in front of her niece.

"What is going on here?" she demanded, crossing her arms over her chest. "Why are you harassing my niece?"

Burt grinned at Rose. "This is your niece?" he asked, gesturing at the camera crew to capture Rose on video. "Ma'am, what do you have to say about the allegations that she murdered Heather Blackwood?"

Aunt Rose squinted at him. "My niece didn't have anything to do with that woman's death," she announced. "She is innocent."

Burt looked at her, his smile widening. "How can you be so sure?" he asked.

Aunt Rose shook her head. "I think you all need to get off of my property," she stated firmly. "This is not the time or place to question my niece. She has already done her time at the police station and does not need any more questions."

Burt's eyes grew large. "You just said she has done time?" he questioned Rose. "So your niece has a criminal history? Is this perhaps not the first murder she has committed?"

Rose frowned. "That isn't what I meant, and you know it," she spat angrily. "Please don't twist my words around."

Tracy leaned into her aunt's ear. "Let's go inside," she suggested. "I don't want this to become a bigger deal than it has to be."

She took her aunt by the elbow and tried to push past Burt and the camera crew. "Please move," she asked as they did not get out of her way.

"Tracy, it was reported that you have had it out for Heather for a long time," Burt called out. "Can you tell us about that?"

"Heather Hampton was a piece of work in high school," Tracy replied, not looking at Burt. "But I don't even know her anymore. I haven't seen her in ten years."

"You heard it here first, everyone," Burt turned to face the camera, his face grim. "Tracy Adams has gone on camera in this tell-all interview and declared that she thought Heather Blackwood was trouble."

Tracy spun around. "I didn't say that," she roared, balling her hands into fists. "I didn't say anything like that. Heather was a jerk in high school, but that doesn't mean I killed her."

"Tracy Adams, killer, calls her victim a jerk," Burt stoically reported as he gripped his microphone tightly. "Tracy, is there anything else you have to say?"

Before she could respond, Tiffany darted out the front door. "Move aside," she yelled as she reached for Rose and Tracy, grabbing them by their wrists and pulling them inside of the flower shop, locking the door behind her.

"They're still out there," Tracy moaned.

"Close the blinds," Aunt Rose ordered. "And turn off the lights. "They want a show, and we aren't going to give one to them."

They scurried around the shop, locking all the doors, windows, and closing every curtain. They flipped off the lights, and after a few minutes, they heard the reporter and camera crew leaving.

"That was Burt Brock," Tiffany exhaled as they leaned against the front counter. "He's super famous; my dad watches his show every night. What's he doing here?"

"Trying to get a good scoop," Tracy complained as she buried her head in her hands. "They are going to ruin my reputation; can you *believe* they sent a national news crew here to cover Heather's death? Everyone is going to see that footage and think I did it."

Aunt Rose wrinkled her nose. "Why do you think they are here?"

Tracy furrowed her brow. "Heather's dad is well known in the town and in the region," she informed them. "I wonder if that's why the news team came here?"

"Who knows," Tiffany chimed in. "But Rose? I think we need to close for the day. Those people are gone, but they're gonna come back. They're ruthless."

Tracy hung her head. "This is a mess," she moaned as Aunt Rose wrapped an arm around her shoulder. "And I don't know how I am going to get out of it."

"We will figure it out," Aunt Rose promised her. "Together, Tracy; we are family, and we are a team. I won't let you lose everything because of a sticky situation, I promise."

Tracy turned to hug her aunt. "Thank you," she murmured into Rose's shoulder.

Aunt Rose returned the hug as Tiffany put her hands on her narrow hips. "The first thing we need to do is figure out who did it," the teenager declared. "We have to clear her name."

Tracy nodded. "We do," she agreed. "But where do we start?"

"That Marshall Street house," Aunt Rose whispered. "We need to find out why Next Move sent you there."

"Let's give them a call," Tiffany suggested. "We can use your new phone, Rose."

Rose pulled the phone out of her pocket and dialed the number for Next Move.

"Next Move Real Estate Company, Fern Grove Branch. This is Bethany speaking," a young woman's voice greeted them.

"Hi, Bethany. This is Rose from In Season. How are you doing today?"

"Rose, nice to hear from you," Bethany chirped. "I'm well, thank you. What can I do for you today?"

Rose looked at Tiffany and Tracy. "I have a little follow up question about an order your office called in this morning," she explained. "For a house at 111 Marshall Street?"

"Marshall Street?" Bethany asked. "Did I hear that correctly?"

"Yes, you did."

Bethany sighed. "Rose, we don't currently have any houses on Marshall Street in our registry," she shared. "I can double check, but I'm sure we aren't contracted with anyone on Marshall Street at the moment."

"Can you double check?" Rose pressed. "It's very important."

"Not a problem," Bethany assured her. "Give me a second; I'm going to put you on hold."

The call switched over to an instrumental cover of 'Hound Dog' by Elvis Presley. "I love this song," Tiffany gushed, and Rose shot her a dark look.

Bethany returned a moment later. "Rose?"

"Still here!"

"I'm sorry to tell you, but we don't have any houses under contract on that street," Bethany informed her. "Did you perhaps mean Markle Street? Matthew Avenue? We have a few places under contract on Marshland Boulevard? Is that what you meant?"

Aunt Rose looked at Tracy. "No," she told her. "It was 111 Marshall Street."

Bethany clucked. "It must be a misunderstanding. Do you know who called you?"

"They didn't give a name," Tracy muttered.

"What? That's okay," Bethany assured her. "I'll just check our call log. What time did they call? And what number did they reach out to?"

"Eight thirty," Tracy guessed. "And my phone number is 206-089-1217."

"Okay," Bethany told them. "Okay, well, I'm looking at the call log, and we don't have anything around that time, nor do we have any calls today to that number."

The color drained from Tracy's face as she realized what this meant. "Next Move didn't call to send me to that house," she whispered as Aunt Rose politely ended the call with Bethany.

"If it wasn't Next Move," Tiffany began. "Then who sent you there?"

"I have no idea," Tracy breathed as goosebumps raised all over her arms and back. "Someone wanted me at that house," she whispered. "Someone wanted *me* to pay for what *they* did to Heather."

8

T hat evening, she opened her phone to find dozens of calls and texts from Warren.

Are you okay??

Babe? What happened?

Why aren't you answering?

Tracy? Where ARE you?

She hastily dialed Warren's phone number and felt relief when he answered on the first ring. "Babe…"

"What is going on?" Warren exclaimed. She could hear the worry in his voice. "I've been trying to get ahold of you for hours. Are you alright?"

"I'm fine," she assured him.

"Thank goodness," he commented. "So is everything okay? They wouldn't give me any information when I tried to find you; they are saying this is a huge conflict of interest. My boss threatened to put me on an administrative leave if I kept digging around for details."

She frowned. "That isn't good," she said quietly. "The whole thing isn't good, Warren; they think I did it. They won't tell me if I am a suspect. I was advised to let them know if I was leaving the area."

"WHAT?"

"Yeah…"

He exhaled loudly. "We never officially name suspects in these cases," he shared with her. "But if you were advised to update them on your movement, then you're very likely a suspect."

Her body felt cold as she weighed her fiancé's words. She was a *suspect* in a murder investigation? Tracy felt sick to her stomach; she swallowed, hoping she could keep the nausea that was growing in her stomach at bay.

"Where are you?" Warren asked. "I need to see you."

"I just got home," she told him.

"Stay there," he ordered her. "I'll be by in a few to pick you up. We can grab dinner and talk about how we're going to get you out of this mess."

Tracy felt grateful for her assertive, supportive fiancé; Warren was always there to help her when she needed him, and she was so happy she was not navigating this difficult situation alone.

"Okay, honey," she told him quietly. "I'll see you soon."

They hung up the phone, and Tracy peeled off her outfit, wrinkling her nose as she inhaled the sharp stench of sweat from the sweater she had been wearing. She had experienced so many emotions that day, and she had sweated through her clothes more than once as she had been questioned at the station.

She threw the soiled sweater into her laundry hamper and removed her pants, tossing them into the laundry as well. Knowing she needed to freshen up before seeing Warren, she took a long, hot shower. She tried to relax as the water soaked her body, and she took long inhales and exhales as the steam filled the bathroom.

The shower curtain moved, and she smiled as Mr.

Sydney, her beloved Abyssinian cat, poked his head into the shower. He did not like the water, but sometimes, he would perch on the edge of the bathtub and watch her as she washed up.

"Hi, baby," she greeted him, bending down to kiss him on the head. She blinked as soap got in her eyes, and she quickly turned to wash it out.

"That hurt," she moaned as she turned the shower off and got out, stepping into her blue terry bathrobe. "Mr. Sydney, this is just not my day."

He followed her as she walked into the single bedroom of her apartment, rubbing up against her legs as she stood in front of her closet, trying to decide what to wear. She selected a simple outfit of black stretchy leggings and an oversized peach tunic top. She knew the outfit was not flattering on her short, curvy body (she was drowning in the baggy shirt and knew she looked better in outfits that cinched in at her waist), but she did not care; she was clean, at least, and she was happy to be out of her dirty clothes.

As she surveyed herself in the mirror, she imagined herself in a wedding dress. She had not yet started to look at gowns, but she knew she wanted a sweetheart neckline to show off her bosom, a tight waist to accentuate her curves, and a flowy skirt that she could spin around in. She reached to pile her hair atop her head in a bun, but then shook her head and let her hair fall on her shoulders; she looked better with her hair down, and she imagined she would have a gorgeous barrette or clip to pull it out of her eyes on her wedding day.

"What are *you* going to wear to our wedding, Mr. Sydney?" she clucked as the cat came over to walk between her legs. "You *are* my best man; I can't imagine my wedding day without you."

An hour later, Tracy and Warren were seated across the

table from each other at Beijing Beef. Warren hadn't wanted to return to where the bad news had seemingly started, but Tracy had been craving Chinese food, and she thought the low-key, relaxed restaurant would help take her mind off of the events of the day.

Warren reached across the table and took her hand. "I can't believe what happened today," he sighed as he stared into her eyes. "You are so brave, Tracy; if I had been arrested and taken to jail like that, I would have been crying like a baby."

She smiled. "I wouldn't say I was brave," she told him. "But I was trying to stay calm; I knew that if I freaked out, I would lose credibility, and I need them to believe my story."

Warren dropped her hand and reached for the menu. "You must be starving," he murmured. "Want me to order for us?"

"That would be great," she sighed, happy Warren was taking charge so she could just relax and enjoy his company. "You know what I like."

She heard the sound of a television click on in the corner and turned around to see a waitress turning on a basketball game for a teenage customer. Warren smiled as he caught her eye; he loved basketball, and she knew he would be sneaking peeks at the game as they ate.

"Hey," she said sharply. "Focus on *me*, babe; I'm more important than State Ohio University and University of Indiana basketball."

Warren clutched his heart, feigning shock and distress. "Tracy," he began. "First, it's Ohio State and Indiana University. Calling them anything else is blasphemy. Second, I don't know if I can marry a girl who knows nothing about college basketball. You're killing me, honey."

She paled at his words. "Maybe now isn't the best time to say I'm killing you," she hissed as Warren's face fell.

"Oh, Tracy," he muttered. "I am so sorry."

The familiar jingle of the local news station filled the room, and Tracy saw the game had ended and the evening news was coming on the television. "Oh no," she groaned as the news started.

"Good evening," the announcer, a petite strawberry blonde woman, began. "Tonight, we bring you footage from a scene outside of In Season, a local flower shop."

"Oh gosh," Tracy's eyes widened as Warren's jaw dropped.

"Tracy Adams, who has been said to have connections to the death of Heather Blackwood, was spotted outside of her aunt's shop today. Tracy seemed disoriented and aggressive, and witnesses say she was acting out of the ordinary."

They cut to a clip of Tracy outside of the flower shop. Her eyes looked wild with worry, and in her dirty clothes, she looked disheveled as she glared at the cameras.

"Heather was a jerk," the onscreen Tracy fired at Burt Brock. "She was a piece of work."

In the restaurant, Tracy's face turned red. "That isn't what I said," she told Warren. "Not exactly; they edited this to look a certain way."

A waitress rushed over to the television and turned the volume up. Aunt Rose's voice filled the room. "My niece did her time."

"She meant that I talked to the officers," Tracy explained as Warren shook his head. "At the station. They've edited it to make it seem like I've been in prison or something."

The story ended, and one of the waiters, a ginger-haired man with a tall mohawk, approached the table. "Hey," he greeted them, though his face was dark. "You certainly look familiar," he said to Tracy.

She ducked down in her seat as Warren handed the menus to him. "We'll do the orange chicken, spring rolls, an order of the pork dumplings, egg drop soup, and two waters, please."

The waiter sneered at them. "I'm not sure I can do that," he told them. "We don't serve *killers* here at Beijing Beef."

Warren raised an eyebrow. "What did you just say?"

"I asked if you wanted the orange chicken to be spicy or mild," the waiter smirked. "Or if you'd like some jail time with your order..."

"That's it," Warren grumbled as he quickly rose from his seat, took the waiter by the shoulders, and shoved him into the wall. "Why don't you say all of that to my face, man? You wanna run your mouth about my fianceé? Great. Then do it so I can hear you and not under your breath like a little baby."

The waiter blinked. "Hey man, I was just playing around," he promised as Tracy rose from her seat and dashed over to Warren. "Sorry to bother you. I know *you* weren't the one who killed that lady. It's your fiancé's fault."

Warren pushed him harder into the wall, and the force sent the waiter's head back. He struck the wall with a loud crack. "Maybe you were the killer," the waiter said sharply as he shook his head. "That hurt, dude. Get off of me."

Tracy tugged on Warren's jacket. "You are making a scene," she warned him. "Get away from him. We need to get out of here."

"No one is gonna talk to my girl like that."

She glared at him. "Do you want to end up in jail or on the news? Babe, this is ridiculous. Come on."

He sighed. "Ok, okay."

He obediently followed her back to their table, and they sat down. Tracy felt annoyed; it was nice to have Warren stand up for her in a show of chivalry, but she did not want him to get into trouble for responding to a stupid comment made by a boy who was barely through puberty.

"I'm sorry," he offered as he planted a smile on his face. "I'll behave."

"Good," she told him. "I've gotten enough attention for a lifetime. I don't need you to get into trouble, too."

"I know," he agreed, reaching over to squeeze her hand. "I won't let it happen again. I just hate when people are rude to the people I love. And you are the person I love the most."

Despite feeling irritated, she felt her heart soar. "Babe," she murmured, squeezing his hand. "I love you."

Suddenly, she became distracted; she could just make out the sound of sirens outside, and she felt nervous as the wailing drew closer. Within a moment, two police officers rushed into the restaurant and after speaking with the hostess, they approached their table.

"Hey guys," Warren greeted them. "You grabbing some dinner?"

The female officer shook her head. "Nope," she told him. "I'm sorry to do this, Officer, but you're under arrest, Warren."

"For what?"

"Assault," the other officer stated. "We received an urgent call from the restaurant and heard you were harassing a waiter. We can't have that, man. You know that. You're under arrest, and we're taking you to the station right now."

9

The next morning, Tracy woke up with a splitting headache and a bad attitude. She had not yet heard from Warren; she had gone to the police station, but they would not let her see him. She had waited there until four in the morning, and now, five hours later, as she checked her cell phone, she saw she had no missed calls from him. She took a deep breath, forcing herself to believe that perhaps no news was good news, and that Warren was home and asleep in his own bed, too tired to have called.

As she got ready for work, she wondered about her future; was she going to be charged with murder? Was the fairytale wedding she had dreamed of having with Warren still going to happen? Everything felt uncertain, and a cloud of dread washed over her as she applied her makeup and dressed in a plain pair of dark wash jeans and a pink sweater with bell sleeves.

She was fifteen minutes late to work, but Aunt Rose said nothing, only handing her her apron and giving her a nod. Tracy tied the apron around her waist, feeling irritable as she reviewed the list of orders she had to fill for the day.

Just before lunchtime, a middle-aged woman came into the shop. She was holding a yappy little dog, and the animal would not stop barking. Tracy frowned as the woman approached the counter; the dog looked angry and was wriggling in the woman's arms, and she did not want to get bitten.

"Can I help you?" she asked curtly.

"Yes, dear," the woman said kindly. "I would like a bouquet. I am visiting my granddaughter at the hospital; she broke her arm, and I think she would love some flowers."

"What kind of flowers?" Tracy asked flatly.

"Ummm... what would you recommend?" the woman smiled.

"You could do some violas. They are in season. Or maybe some Glory of the Snow."

The woman's face brightened. "That sounds nice. What do Glory of the Snow flowers look like? What color?"

Tracy furrowed her brow. "They're white," she said flatly. "Like snow."

Aunt Rose hurried over and shooed Tracy away. "Here, why don't I do a little bouquet of pansies? They are in season and the colors are just beautiful, especially for a little girl."

Aunt Rose assembled the flowers, and the woman paid for the bouquet. "Have a lovely day," Rose called out as the woman waved goodbye.

She turned to her niece. "I know you are under a lot of stress, but that is no excuse for poor customer service. You acted so disinterested toward that customer, Tracy. It was unbecoming."

Tracy hung her head, feeling the sting of shame flood her body. "I'm sorry," she muttered. "It was a long night. Warren was arrested."

Her aunt's jaw dropped. "What? Warren was *arrested*? They think he had a part in Heather's murder?"

"No," she told her. "But someone was making fun of *me* for it, and he shoved the guy against a wall. I don't know if any charges have been made against him, but it was a hard night for the both of us."

Aunt Rose undid her apron. "We're leaving," she told Tracy. "You are not in the right frame of mind to serve customers. Let's grab a cup of coffee and start over later."

Tiffany popped her head out of the backroom. "Can I come?"

"I need you to hold down the fort," Aunt Rose informed her. "We'll be back in an hour or so. I'll bring a latte and a muffin back for you."

"Deal," Tiffany grinned. "By the way, can I pop out to grab some lunch when I've finished cleaning the storage room?"

Aunt Rose nodded her approval as they left the shop and made their way in silence to Grind it Out. When they arrived, Tracy sat down in the back corner booth, thankful for its remote location in the coffee shop.

Aunt Rose came to the table a few moments later holding two cinnamon spice lattes. "They're a new addition to the menu," she told Tracy. "Drink up, dear. You look like you need a boost."

Tracy took a sip. "This is good," she said in spite of herself. "I think this is just what I needed to bring myself back to life."

"I hoped you would say that." Aunt Rose smiled. "How about this? We'll finish our coffees, go back to work, and tomorrow, we'll do a little spa day at my house. I can give you a manicure and a pedicure to perk you up."

Tracy's heart warmed. Her aunt loved her so much; Aunt Rose had raised her after her parents had died, and she loved Tracy like her own. "That would be wonderful," she told her. "Thank you."

They chatted for a bit, and Tracy saw her aunt's mug was empty. "I'll go get another one for you."

She got up and went to stand in line behind two teenage girls who were buried in their cell phones. "At least they aren't paying attention to me," she thought.

Out of the corner of her eye, she saw a man staring at her. He looked familiar, but she couldn't quite place him. Had he been a customer at the flower shop? She gave him a small smile, but he looked down at his leather shoes before they could make eye contact.

When it was her turn to order, she waved to Jurgen, the owner of the coffee shop. He flashed her a large smile, and she sighed in relief, glad that he was treating her as he always did. "What can I get for you?"

"My aunt needs a refill," she explained. "Hey, Jurgen? Who is that man over there?"

"Which one?"

"The guy in the blue sweater and leather shoes."

Jurgen peered over to where the man was sitting alone. "I don't know," he shrugged. "Is he bothering you?"

"No," she promised. "I'm fine."

"Good," he nodded as he took her five-dollar bill and counted out change. "I'm so sorry for all the craziness you've had to deal with, Tracy. You're a wonderful woman, and shame on anyone who thinks you had something to do with that Blackwood woman's death. It's ridiculous."

"That is so kind of you to say," she told him as her eyes crinkled into a smile. "Jurgen, I wish more people thought the way you did. I didn't know people in Fern Grove were so gullible; they just believe anything they hear on the news. It's awful."

He shook his head. "People should have faith in each other," he complained. "I know you're a nice lady and you wouldn't hurt a fly. Hang in there, Tracy. The truth will come out, and it will all be okay."

She thanked him for his kindness and the coffee and made her way back to the booth where her aunt was waiting for her. As she walked by a table of two mothers rocking their babies, she heard them whisper her name. She stared straight ahead, but the same thing happened as she passed a table filled with older ladies playing cards.

"What's wrong?" Aunt Rose asked when she returned. "I thought you were feeling better, dear."

Tracy set the mug of coffee in front of her aunt. "People think I killed Heather Blackwood," she said sharply. "The people in this town—my town—really think I ended someone's life. It makes me sick. People are gossiping about me and staring at me. Like him!"

She turned to point at the man in the blue sweater, but his table was empty.

"I don't see anyone staring at you," Aunt Rose gently assured her. "I think you're projecting, honey. No one is staring at you or watching you…"

"Oh…."

She felt her stomach churn. There *had* been a man in a blue sweater in the coffee shop, and he *had* been watching her. Or had he? Tracy gulped. She had already lost her spotless reputation. Was she losing her mind as well?

10

As Tracy and her aunt walked back to In season, a torrential downpour began.

"I'm getting soaked," Tracy complained as a car drove by and hit a puddle, sending a wall of water crashing toward them. "I'm gonna have to run home and change."

"Me too," Aunt Rose laughed.

Tracy eyed her. "Why are you laughing? This weather is gross."

Aunt Rose shrugged. "Look at it this way, Tracy: no rain, no flowers. Sometimes, things are gross and awful, but in the end, they lead to beautiful beginnings."

Tracy rolled her eyes. "You should be in charge of writing fortunes for fortune cookies," she observed as they hurried along in the rain. "That was a nice little saying."

Another car drove by, but instead of passing them, it slowed to a stop. "There is the killer," a girl's voice shrieked, and then the car sped away, splashing even more water on Tracy and Rose.

"This is the worst day," she groaned, but Aunt Rose took her hand.

"Let's just get out of the rain," she urged her niece. "This isn't the end of the world, Tracy, I promise. I know it's hard and things feel scary, but the rain will stop, and the sun will shine again."

"I hope you are right," Tracy murmured as Rose led her inside of Becky Sue Styles, a local hair salon.

The salon was quiet; in the corner, a young woman was having her hair trimmed, but no other customers were present. Soft rock hits played from speakers mounted in the walls, and Tracy was glad it wasn't crowded.

"Well, look what the cat dragged in."

Becky Sue, the owner of the salon, sashayed over to them, a smile on her face. Becky Sue had moved back to Fern Grove from Hollywood a few years prior to care for her ailing father, and she was unlike anyone Tracy had ever met. She was beautiful and kind, and she exuded grace and glamor.

"Can I get you gals some tea? You look like you need it," she commented as she surveyed their wet clothes. "Maybe a towel?"

"That sounds great," Rose told her.

"I'll be right back."

She returned a moment later with two cups of tea and a set of towels. "You two dry off and make yourselves comfortable; this storm is terrible, and I am so pleased you ducked in."

Rose smiled. "You are too kind."

Becky Sue frowned. "I've been worried about you, Tracy. How are you doing? I can't believe what they're saying about you in town."

Tracy raised an eyebrow. "What are they saying?"

Becky Sue shook her head. "I had the news on in here, and some of my clients were chiming in about how you murdered Heather Blackwood. It's quite silly, really; anyone who knows you, knows how lovely you are. I just can't believe it's escalated to this level."

Tracy was annoyed to hear people were gossiping about her, but grateful to know Becky Sue disapproved of their stories. "It's crazy," she agreed.

Becky Sue led them to a mauve leather couch in her waiting area. "Sit, sit."

They sat down, holding their cups of tea close to their faces. Tracy inhaled the hot steam, enjoying the way it warmed her face.

"I just can't believe they haven't accused her husband. I watch a lot of crime shows, and they *always* blame the husband," Becky Sue said incredulously. "Then again, Heather and Drew were such a lovely couple; Drew grew up on the wrong side of the tracks in Chicago, but managed to earn a football scholarship to Notre Dame. He and Heather met there, and now, they raise money for youth sports teams in bad neighborhoods. Well, at least, they did before…"

"Before she died," Tracy finished.

"Exactly. They were philanthropists and a power couple, that's for sure. Rumor was that Heather was planning to come back to Fern Grove and run for office; there is an open seat in the state government for our district, and I heard Heather wanted it. Her parents' money and connections wouldn't have made it hard for her to win."

Tracy bit her lip. "Wow, I didn't know that about her."

Becky Sue nodded. "Heather was tough, but she had an indomitable spirit that could have helped a lot of people. Poor Drew. I don't know what he is going to do without her."

Tracy shook her head. "Grow a backbone?"

Becky Sue looked over at her with a shocked expression on her face. "Did you really just say that?" she asked. "Seriously?"

"What? Say what? No," Tracy stumbled on her words, but Becky saw right through her.

"I can only imagine getting blamed for Mrs. Blackwood's death has been hard on you, but there is no need to speak disrespectfully of the dead."

"She didn't mean it," Aunt Rose insisted. "Becky Sue, Tracy is just exhausted. Can you imagine what she is going through right now?"

Becky Sue stood up. "I think you two should go," she stated firmly. "Please leave my shop, and don't come back until you've learned some manners, Tracy."

Tracy held up her hands. "I'm sorry," she apologized, her face pinched. "Really, I am so sorry. That was uncalled for and in poor taste, and I shouldn't have said it."

"Please go," Becky Sue retorted. "Now."

It was still raining when they stepped outside, but the dark clouds had grown lighter, and the wind was quieting down. They trudged through the wet streets in silence; Tracy could not even look at her aunt, imagining how furious she must be with her.

When they arrived at In Season, they found the front door wide open. "That's odd," Aunt Rose commented as they walked inside.

She gasped. The entire front room of the shop was flooded; an inch of water covered the antique wood floors.

"Oh, my word," Tracy muttered as she sprang into action, running around to the electronics and unplugging the computer, the cash register, and the printer. "What happened? Where is Tiffany?"

"I don't know... Oh, I remember! She must have gone out to grab some lunch," Aunt Rose cried. "But someone has been in here. Look!"

Tracy turned around. The door handle had been broken

and there were shards of glass on the floor. She dashed outside to see if there were any more clues to what had happened. She gasped. On the east wall of the shop was a piece of graffiti. In blood-red letters, a phrase was written:

A murderer works here!

11

Tracy was beside herself as she was interviewed at the shop by a police officer who looked like he couldn't have cared less to be there.

"What was on the security footage? Did you see anything?" the officer asked as he stifled a yawn and leaned back in his chair.

"We don't have security cameras," she informed him. "We're a small flower shop; we've never had any issues before."

He snapped his gum. "Do you have any enemies, Miss Adams?"

"Enemies?" she asked in shock.

He nodded. "Anyone you can think of who would want to scare you?"

She frowned. "Absolutely not," she said firmly. "Besides this Heather Blackwood fiasco, I've never had a lick of trouble in this town."

He raised an eyebrow. "Heather Blackwood? Oh, yes. You're *that* Tracy Adams…"

She bit her lip. "Excuse me?"

"Your name sounded familiar, and now I remember why," he muttered as he rose to his feet. "Just watch your back, Miss Adams. And maybe install a camera or two around here. My team is examining the evidence, but whoever came over here and broke into your shop didn't leave a lot behind."

She sighed. "So, you're just going to let this one go?"

"That is not what I said," he countered. "Look, Miss Adams, I think you should just keep your head down. It seems like that's the best course of action for you at this time, don't you think? You and Warren--"

She stared at him. "Is there any news? Is he okay?"

The officer shrugged. "I shouldn't have mentioned him," he apologized as he moved toward the door. "My apologies. I'm not at liberty to discuss other cases."

As he turned to leave, he waved. "Have a nice day," he told her. "Stay safe."

Tracy sat alone in the front room. The water had been pumped out of the flower shop, but the hardwood floors were ruined; they were soggy and warped, and her heart broke at how much it would cost to replace them.

"Tracy," Aunt Rose cried as she ran into the shop. "Are you okay? I had to run home and fetch my insurance information after I spoke with the officers, but I'm here now."

"It's all my fault," Tracy hung her head sadly as her aunt embraced her. "If it weren't for me, none of this would have happened."

Aunt Rose shook her head vigorously. "Don't say that," she scolded her niece. "Someone chose to come into this shop and deface it. You had nothing to do with it. Do not blame yourself, Tracy."

"The floors are ruined," Tracy continued, burying her face in her hands. "Our gorgeous floors."

"Which is why we have insurance," Aunt Rose smiled. "Tracy, as long as you and Tiffany are safe, I don't care what happens to this building; people are what matters, not the place itself. You girls are safe and everyone is okay, and I am just grateful we have the means and resources to fix this mess and move on."

Tracy leaned into her aunt's embrace. "I love you," she whispered. "I am so grateful for you."

"Mutual feeling, dear," her aunt assured her as she playfully tugged on a strand of Tracy's hair. "Did they mention anything about your sweetheart? Poor Warren."

The hair on Tracy's arms stood up. "Warren," she fretted as she pulled her cell phone out of her pocket. "I need to text him."

She punched the message into her cell phone.

Honey? I'm worried about you. Something bad happened at the shop. Call me.

She sent the message, but he did not instantly respond. "I wonder if something is wrong," she worried as she looked at her aunt. "I should give him a call."

She dialed his number, and it went straight to voicemail.

"I'm sure everything is fine," her aunt reassured her. "Let's get things straightened up around here and we can open the shop. That will help calm you down."

"You want to open the shop when your floor is ruined?" Tracy asked incredulously. "Are you sure?"

Her aunt's eyes sparkled. "People still need flowers, darlin'. Don't you worry; the floor just looks bad. That doesn't mean people can't walk on it."

They cleaned up the front counters and swept all the shards of glass into a dustpan, straightened up the buckets of flowers along the walls, and turned the lights on. "There," Aunt Rose smiled as she surveyed their work. "See? Besides the yucky floors, we are *back* in action."

They got to work, starting with usual tasks of the day, such as watering the flowers in their back stockroom, counting the money in the cash register, and printing receipts for online orders. An hour passed, but no one came into the shop.

"I wonder if they think we're closed?" Tracy wondered aloud.

"I know what it is," her aunt grinned. "We didn't flip our sign or put our outdoor sign on the sidewalk in front of the shop. It still says we are closed. Will you go take care of that?"

"Sure thing."

Tracy flipped the indoor sign in the window and carried the wooden sign outdoors. She felt her chest pound as she glanced up at the wall. "Oh, no…"

She rushed back inside. "I know why no one is coming in," she explained. "The graffiti is still outside. We forgot all about it."

Aunt Rose's eyes widened. "That explains it," she confirmed. "Come on, dear. Let's get a bucket and a mop and get to work on that nasty message."

They gathered the supplies and went outside. The graffiti was written in ugly block letters, and Tracy cringed as she lifted a mop to the wall and began to pump it back and forth. "We might have to hire a professional," she groaned. "This will never come off."

"Never say never," her aunt advised her. "We'll get it done."

They worked hard, using all of their might to work away at the red lettering that took up nearly three feet of space on the wall. "Maybe we could paint over it?" Tracy asked.

"No, it needs to go," Aunt Rose told her.

As they worked, Tracy heard a sound from behind her. She stopped, feeling someone's gaze. She quickly turned around and saw the man with the blue sweater from Grind it Out. He was ten or fifteen feet behind her, but it was clear he was watching them.

"Hey," she called out. "Do you need something?"

He said nothing, and she poked her aunt. "Hey, that guy is watching us," she mouthed as Aunt Rose peered behind them.

"He is? Why? Who is that?"

"I don't know," Tracy told her. "But I'm going to find out."

Tracy gasped as she saw her fiancé for the first time after the eventful episode at the restaurant. Warren looked horrible; he had dark circles under his eyes, his hair was messy, and he was wearing a pair of sweatpants that were ripped at the knees. As he opened the door, Tracy wrinkled her nose; there was a sour odor coming from inside the house.

"Honey?" she murmured as she glanced inside. "Are you alright? I've been trying to get a hold of you. Why haven't you been returning my calls?"

Warren's dog ran up and stuck his nose into Tracy's face. "Hi, buddy," she greeted him, bending down and scratching his ears. "Are you taking good care of your daddy? It looks like he needs it..."

Warren ran a hand through his greasy hair and sighed. "I'm sorry," he offered as he led her into his living room. "I haven't been in a great state of mind, dear."

She looked around. Empty takeout boxes covered the kitchen table, there were piles of clothes on the floor, and the large succulent she had bought for his last birthday was dead.

"I can see that," she said gently. "I'm so glad you are home; how long did they keep you at the station?"

His face darkened. "Overnight," he spat furiously. "And they put me on unpaid administrative leave because of the altercation between myself and that waiter. I'll lose my job if he doesn't drop the charges. What am I gonna do if that happens? I've worked my tail off to get to where I am today; I did everything right, Tracy... at least until last night. I worked hard, made good grades in school, did well in college, aced the police academy... and now, it could all be taken from me. What am I gonna do?"

She bit her lip. "I don't know," she told him. "But I know what you can do for now: why don't you shower and put on some fresh clothes. I'll throw together some dinner for us, and maybe we can go for a walk and get you some fresh air."

He shrugged. "I don't know," he frowned.

"Come on," she urged him. "You'll feel better, I promise."

Warren complied, and when Tracy heard the sound of the shower turning on, she sprang into action, gathering the empty takeout boxes and the dead plant, stuffing them into the trash. She wiped off his kitchen counter and the table, careful to get every speck of old food and dirt off of the surfaces. She ran into his room and made his bed, opened the curtains, and then returned to the kitchen where she opened the refrigerator.

There was barely any food, but Tracy spotted a bag of romaine lettuce, a red onion, a lemon, and an avocado. She quickly threw together a salad, using the lemon to make an easy dressing, and she set the table for two.

When Warren emerged from the bathroom, he looked like a new person; his face was freshly shaven, his hair was slicked back with product, and he smelled like the cologne Tracy had gotten him for Christmas.

"What's all this?" he asked as he came into the kitchen dressed in a pair of clean jeans and a crew neck sweatshirt.

"It's dinner," she replied cheerfully. "You look like you could use a home-cooked meal, dear."

"You didn't have to do all of this."

"I *get* to do all of this," she smiled. "I'm going to be your *wife*, Warren. This is what partners do for each other."

They sat down at the table and began to eat their salads. "Thanks for putting all of this together," he thanked her between bites. "I don't think salad has ever tasted this good."

When they finished their meal, she checked the weather and clapped her hands with excitement. "It's not going to rain," she told her fiancé. "Let's get outside. I think the change of scenery will really help you."

He sighed. "I don't want to, babe…"

"Please? For me?"

He rose to his feet and walked to his bedroom, returning five minutes later with a jacket. "Okay, okay. Let's go."

They left the house and walked in silence for a few moments. She glanced over and saw his face was dark, and she wrapped an arm around his waist, snuggling into his arms as they walked.

"I talked with a vendor today," she chattered as they strolled along. "The string light people are charging way too much for lights to hang over the reception. I thought we could just do them ourselves. What did Pastor Butler say when you asked if he would officiate? Have you had a chance to ask him yet, babe?"

Warren furrowed his brow. "I can't really do wedding talk right now," he said matter-of-factly. "Sorry. I have too much on my mind."

"No problem," she forced herself to say with a smile. "Wedding talk can wait."

"Thanks."

She racked her brain for subjects that would cheer him up; Warren was clearly disappointed to be on administrative leave from his job, and Tracy imagined his night in jail was one of the worst of his life.

"Are you ready to be a cat dad?" she finally asked, trying to keep the mood light. "Mr. Sydney adores you and your dog. I hope we are one big happy family when we get married."

His face broke into a smile. "At last!" Tracy thought to herself.

"I think we'll all get along," he promised her. "Mr. Sydney and I need to spend more time together; when we get married, will we give him my last name? Or is Sydney his last name?"

Tracy giggled. "Great questions," she grinned. "I'm not sure…. what do you think is the best thing to do?"

"Mr. Sydney is a prestigious name," Warren said, a reverent look on his face. "But maybe we add my last name?"

Tracy wrinkled her nose. "Hmmm… I'll need to run that by Mr. Sydney. He gets a bit touchy about these things."

"I know, I know," he replied, chuckling. "What if we hyphenate Mr. Sydney's name? Give him yours and mine?"

"I like it," she told him, taking his hand in hers and giving it a squeeze. "We'll have to do a little date for him and the dog soon; they are going to be brothers, after all."

"That will be fun," he agreed.

An hour later, as Tracy arrived home at her apartment, her phone vibrated. She looked at the screen and saw it was her aunt calling.

"Tracy?"

"Aunt Rose, what's up?" she asked as she answered the call.

Her aunt took a deep breath. "I have some news," she whispered. "Next Move just called me."

Her stomach churned. "For real? Or the fake Next Move?"

"It's the real Next Move," her Aunt assured her. "I got the caller's name and looked her up on my computer as we spoke; it's legit."

"What did they want?"

"They have an update about the caller," her aunt whispered. "The person who called and sent you to the Marshall Street house."

"What? What's the update?" Tracy asked, her heart racing.

"Come to the flower shop," Aunt Rose told her. "I don't think we should talk about this over the phone anymore."

"I can be there in five minutes."

They hung up the call, and Tracy took a deep breath. Someone *knew* something about what had happened to Heather Blackwood, and she hoped it was going to be the breakthrough they needed.

13

Tracy raced down to the flower shop, pumping her arms as she jogged through the streets of Fern Grove. She *had* to figure out what was going on; her reputation and the success of In Season depended on it.

As she rounded the corner, her phone rang again.

"Aunt Rose? What's up? I'm almost there."

Her aunt sighed. "I need you to do a favor for me," she asked.

"Anything."

"I need apple cider vinegar from the market to clean the planters," she told her. "Can you stop and grab it?"

Tracy frowned. "Why don't I come to the shop first, and then I can go to the market, Aunt Rose."

"No, I need the apple cider vinegar now," her aunt murmured. "Please, Tracy? It will only take five minutes."

Tracy took a deep breath, then pasted a smile on her face. "Fine," she nodded. "Fine. Do you need the big bottle?"

"The jumbo size," her aunt informed her. "And maybe a pack of gum. Thanks, doll."

Tracy turned on her heel and set off for the market. She

tried to stifle her frustration; didn't her aunt know she was desperate for information about the Heather Blackwood situation?

When she arrived at the market, she saw the worker stocking shelves give her a dark look. "Yikes," she thought to herself. "I guess I won't go down that aisle..."

She wandered over to the produce section. She was hungry, and a banana sounded like the perfect snack. She examined a few bunches but did not select one; all of them looked too green, and she would rather go hungry than eat a sour banana.

As she went in search of the apple cider vinegar, she bumped into an elderly woman holding a shopping basket. The woman shot her a nasty look, and Tracy's eyes widened. "Sorry, I didn't see you there," she apologized.

"Clearly," the woman spat.

Tracy watched her hurry away. "That was so rude," she sighed as the woman turned the corner. "Does everyone in this town seriously think I killed Heather Blackwood? It's so unfair."

She wandered to the baking aisle and selected a sixty-four-ounce bottle of apple cider vinegar that she knew her aunt would love. As she held it close to her chest on the way to the check-out line, she saw another woman shooting her a glare. The woman had short brown hair and a round face, and her eyes were filled with disgust.

"Hi," Tracy said to her with sass, batting her eyelashes and holding her head high. "Can I help you?"

The woman said nothing, and Tracy quickly paid for the bottle and hurried out of the store. She rushed to the flower shop and burst through the front door, eager to hear what her aunt had to say.

"There you are," her aunt smiled at her. "Thanks for running the errand for me; we've been in desperate need of

ACV for a week, and the thought struck me when we got off the phone earlier."

"No worries," Tracy told her. "Has the shop been busy?"

"No customers," Aunt Rose replied, looking glum.

"The graffiti looks better," Tracy commented. "You can barely see the shadow from all of our scrubbing."

"Oh, good," her aunt cried in relief. "I was worried it was still visible."

Tracy stared into her aunt's face. "So, what's the big update?" she asked, her eyes alert and her hands nearly shaking from the anticipation. "What did Next Move say?"

Aunt Rose bit her lip. "I don't know if you should be that excited," she cautioned her niece. "They called to let me know they are going through their logbooks again to find out if the call about the Marshall house was made from their office or not. They are also working with the phone company to get more information, too."

Tracy furrowed her brow. "Have they called with any information about the logbooks?" she asked eagerly. "Did they give you a timeline of when to expect information?"

"Not really," her aunt told her. "They were very kind, though; the girl on the phone, Kathy, was so nice and friendly."

"That's great," she replied, trying not to drown in the deep frustration that was quickly overcoming her. "I'm glad you had a nice conversation."

Aunt Rose met her gaze. "Just try to relax, dear," she urged her. "It will all be okay in the end, Tracy."

Tracy balled her hands into fists. "I don't know if it will," she protested. "I'm going to go down there; surely Next Move will give me some information if I show up in person."

"What? You want to go to Next Move?"

She nodded. "I think it's a good idea," she declared,

placing her hands on her hips and holding her head high. "I need to clear my name, and I think they can help me do it."

Her aunt put her hand on her shoulder. "Don't you think you should just wait?" she asked. "Next Move told me they were working on it, Tracy. There is no rush."

She stared at her. "There is a rush," she argued. "My reputation is at stake, Aunt Rose. I want to fix things for myself, and for *us*. The shop is going to suffer if my name is not cleared."

"I think this is a bad idea."

Tracy crossed her arms. "We cannot continue our partnership with Next Move until they help us get out of this mess," she insisted. "I'm going down there, and that's that."

She hurried out of the shop, throwing on her coat as she exited the building. Tracy felt angry, hurt, and very much alone; didn't *anyone* want to see her get out of the mess she was in? Why was she having to do all of the difficult work herself?

As she strode through town, she noticed passersby were avoiding her; people were literally walking to the other side of the street when she neared them, and she felt her heart ache. What if she was not well received at Next Move? Had Aunt Rose been right? Perhaps marching over there when she was worked up was not the greatest idea.

She was struck with another thought; what if the answers to her problems were not with Next Move, but with the house on Marshall Street? She turned on her heel and set off in the opposite direction, switching gears as she headed over to the crime scene to see if she could piece together any evidence.

When Tracy arrived, she was disappointed to see two police cars parked in the driveway. An officer was measuring the garage door, and a police photographer was taking photos of the yard. "I don't want to run into them," she thought as she took a step back. "I hope they didn't see me."

Knowing it would be better if she just returned to In Season, she felt her shoulder slump. A car was approaching her, and she ducked her head, not wanting a negative interaction with another Fern Grove resident. Tracy turned around and began walking back downtown, but before she could think, she saw a little girl dart out of the house across the street and start running.

"Puppy!"

Tracy's eyes moved to the left; a dog was digging in the empty lot across the street from the little girl's house, and she watched as the girl dashed toward the animal.

It was getting dark, and she could not tell if the car driving down the road had spotted the girl. "Oh no," she thought as the girl picked up speed and began hurtling herself into the road. Tracy dropped her purse and sprinted toward her, throwing her arms up so the car would see her and stop.

"STOP!" she screamed as she waved frantically, and with a screech, the car came to a halt.

The little girl cowered behind her, and her parents ran out of their house and into the street. "Candace? Candace, are you okay?" the girl's mother asked, scooping her up and kissing her forehead.

"I wanted the doggy," Candace whined, pointing to the dog who was chasing its tail in the empty lot.

Candace's father waved the driver off, and he, his wife, Tracy, and Candace walked to the sidewalk.

"Thank you so much," her mother thanked Tracy. "You saved her life."

"It was nothing," Tracy assured them. "Just a little bit of the right place and the right time."

Her father peered at her closely. "Do we know you?"

She smiled, but then, her face fell; she realized they must recognize her from the news, and she bit her lip. "I work at the flower shop," she offered weakly.

Candace's mother nodded. "Tracy, right? I recognized you from the news."

"I'll just be going," Tracy told them, but Candace's mother stopped her.

"Wait, you don't have to run off," she offered kindly. "Why don't you come over to our house? We need to thank you for saving our little angel, and we just started dinner. Do you care to join us?"

Tracy's face reddened. "Are you sure you want *me* in your home?" she asked. "I'm sure you've heard what they are saying about me."

The girl's mother rolled her eyes. "This town needs to get a grip," she complained. "People in small towns love to cast villains; they'll have someone new to hate sooner than later, Tracy. Don't take it personally."

Tracy smiled. "Thank you," she told her. "I really needed to hear that."

The woman nodded. "So, are you in for dinner? My husband made a mean eggplant lasagna. You will love it."

Tracy shook her head. "I really need to get going," she told them. "But before I do, can I ask a quick question?"

"Anything!"

Tracy took a deep breath. "What do you know about the area? Have you two lived here long?"

Her husband nodded. "We've been here a year," he shared. "We moved here for her job—my wife is a surgeon, and she is in charge of the local hospital now."

"Wow, that is so cool. Congratulations."

She grinned. "Surgery is easier than parenting a toddler, that's for sure."

Her husband continued. "From what we've gathered,

most of these properties are owned by the wealthier Fern Grove folks and a few out of towners."

"What about 111 Marshall Street?" she asked quietly. "Who lives there?"

The woman looked at her husband. "I don't know," she told Tracy. "We haven't seen anyone come in or out, but the grass is always mowed and the house is kept up."

Tracy raised an eyebrow. "So someone must live there…."

The man shrugged. "Or maybe someone just keeps it up, like a housekeeper."

Candace began to fuss in her mother's arms. "We'd best get going," her father smiled. "Are you sure you won't join us for dinner? You are Candace's hero."

"I can't," she apologized. "Next time, though; it was nice to meet you two."

"Nice to meet you," the woman told her. "And hey, check out the library if you want to find some information about that house; surely they'll have records of some sort. And be careful, Tracy. I know that's the house where everything went down. Watch your back; from what my husband and I have seen, people in Fern Grove can be pretty cutthroat. *Especially* rich people like Heather Blackwood."

14

The next morning, Tracy rose bright and early and made her way to the Fern Grove Public Library. She was dressed in a pair of leggings, a knee-length sweatshirt, and a baseball cap in hopes that no one would recognize her, and as she walked into the library, she was relieved that none of the patrons gave her a second glance.

Tracy walked over to a research computer and sat down, putting her purse in the chair beside her so no one would sit too close to her. She opened the browser and began her hunt for information about Heather Blackwood and the house on Marshall Street.

Fifteen minutes into her search, Tracy felt frustrated; the research computer was difficult to navigate, and she was not quite sure what she was looking for. She felt a hint of relief when a librarian approached her, though she was nervous the woman would recognize her.

"You look like you need some help," the woman, a bespectacled older woman smiled. "These research computers can be tricky to use."

She nodded, saying nothing. The woman glanced at her

screen. "Oh, you're looking up town history? We have an archive of documents and papers and photos on the top floor, if that's helpful."

Tracy bit her lip. "I think that would be very helpful," she decided.

"Let me take you up there," the librarian told her, and Tracy logged off of the computer and followed her upstairs.

When they arrived in the archives, Tracy was amazed by the number of documents; the small room was stuffed with bookshelves containing book after book of Fern Grove history, maps of the town, census data, and old, yellowed photographs of the town from the nineteenth century.

"What exactly are you looking for?" the librarian asked as she pulled out a map of Marshall Street that was dated 1955. "History of the neighborhood? We have records of the area dating back to 1821, if you're interested…"

She shook her head. "I need some contemporary data," she shared. "I am hoping to find information about the owners of all the houses on that street from the last ten years or so. Can you help?"

The librarian wrinkled her nose. "That's not the fun stuff," she muttered. "Whoops. I shouldn't have said that. Forgive me…"

She returned the map to its place and retrieved a blue spiral-bound book from a lower shelf. "This might have what you're looking for: the information about all the elitists on Marshall… oh no. Forgive me, I shouldn't have said that."

Tracy stared at her. "What do you mean?"

The librarian shrugged. "Marshall Street used to be a lovely, picturesque historical street," she explained quietly. "My own mother lived there until she passed in 1999. Thank goodness she died before the new crowd came in; all of these rich folks started demolishing the Victorian-era homes in the neighborhood and built massive, modern looking McMansions. It's truly a tragedy."

Tracy saw the hurt in her eyes. "I am so sorry about your mother," she whispered.

"It's nothing," the librarian replied as she shook her head. "I must go. I hope this is what you needed."

Tracy watched as the older woman scurried away. She picked up the blue book and set it down on the large oak table in the middle of the room and began to read. In the book, there was information about each home on Marshall Street, including photographs of the original homes on each lot. She flipped through the pages until she reached 111 Marshall Street.

"This is what I've been trying to find," she thought gleefully as she started reading the heading.

Before she could get far, she heard footsteps behind her. She turned around hastily, but no one was there. "I'm just spooked," she thought as she resumed reading. "Being in this dark, quiet corner of the library has made me jumpy."

"Hey."

She gasped as she registered the deep baritone of a man's voice. She turned around to find the man who had been at Grind it Out staring at her. He was tall and handsome, with a striking jawline, black hair and bright blue eyes, but she barely registered his good looks as she felt her heart pound in her chest.

"Who are you?" she cried. "Why are you following me?"

He crossed his arms over his green cashmere sweater. "You don't know who I am?"

She shook her head.

He sighed. "I'm Drew Blackwood," he informed her. "I was married to Heather."

Her eyes widened. "Oh my gosh," she moaned. "I am so sorry for your loss. I just want you to know that I had nothing to do with Heather's death. I know the news stories are saying I did it, but I promise that I didn't. I'm not a killer. I work in a flower shop. You have to believe me."

He stared at her, his blue eyes filled with disdain. "I don't know what to believe," he muttered. "Heather is *dead*, and I've watched you run around this town over the last week like you had something to hide. "

"So you *have* been following me," she breathed.

"The police haven't charged you, yet, everyone is saying you did it," he told her. "I had to follow you. I need to know the truth."

She clasped her hands together. "Please believe me," she begged him. "I didn't do it. I'm a good person, Drew. I have a fiancé, and pets, and an aunt I adore."

He raised an eyebrow. "I *know*," he hissed. "I know all of these things. For someone who should really be watching her back right now, you don't take a lot of care to lock your doors, close your curtains, or make sure your mail gets inside of your home…"

Fear filled her chest as she stared at him. "You've been watching my house?"

He cocked his head to the side. "I have a *lot* of time on my hands now that Heather is gone," he sighed. "I'm a quiet, simple man, Tracy; I loved Heather, and I did my part in working behind the scenes to get her to where she wanted to go in life. But now, she's gone, and I need to know *who* and *why*."

She nodded. "I understand that you are upset," she said cautiously. "But I didn't do it."

"If you didn't, then who did?" he demanded, taking a step toward her and getting in her face. "If you didn't do it, why does *everyone* in this town think you did?"

"I don't know," she whimpered as she tried to take a step

back but realized a bookshelf was behind her. "I really don't know."

He was so close that she could smell his breath; it reeked of beer, and she cringed as he moved even closer to her. "I work at Next Move too, you know," he informed her, and her face lit up.

"You work at Next Move?"

He nodded. "On the day the police arrested you at the house where Heather's body was found, they took me in for questioning, too."

"The house," she whispered. "On Marshall Street. Did you have someone call me and go there, Drew? Did you call In Season and send me over there?"

Before he could answer, she noticed the faint sound of sirens outside. The sound swelled until it was nearly unbearable, and then they heard the thunder of footsteps on the stairs.

The door to the archives burst open, and six police officers stormed in. Tracy held up her hands in surrender, but they did not even look at her. An officer threw Drew Blackwood to the floor and whipped a pair of handcuffs out of his belt, snapping them on with a flourish.

"What is this?" Drew yelled as he fought against the officer, his body rocking on the hardwood floor. "What is going on?"

"Drew Blackwood?"

"Yes?"

"You are under arrest," the officer told him.

"For what?"

"I think you know, Mr. Blackwood," The officer replied. "You're under arrest for the murder of Heather Blackwood."

15

T racy could hardly breathe. As she pumped her arms and moved her short legs, running toward the flower shop, she wondered if she had completely lost her mind.

Drew Blackwood had been *arrested* for Heather's murder. Drew! Heather's husband. Tracy hated to admit it, but she felt relief flood her chest as she thought about it. This would clear her name and ensure her reputation was restored, wouldn't it?

She bounded into the flower shop and laughed. "You guys won't believe what just happened," she breathed as Aunt Rose and Tiffany stared at her.

"What is going on? Have you been running?" Tiffany raised an eyebrow.

Tracy glanced around the shop. "No customers again?"

"Not a single one."

She grinned. "That's okay, I think our problems may taken a turn for the better."

Her aunt looked at her with confusion in her eyes. "Tracy? What are you talking about?"

"Drew Blackwood," she declared, placing her hands on her hips. "Drew Blackwood, Heather's husband. I just saw him get arrested. The police dragged him out of the library, kicking and screaming. He may have killed his own wife."

"That's wonderful!" Tiffany cried. "Well, not wonderful that his wife is dead, but wonderful that this is gonna blow over for us."

"It is," Aunt Rose agreed. "I was worried about having to cut Tiffany's hours if things didn't improve; we haven't had any customers in nearly a week, and our accounts are emptying quickly."

"You were gonna cut my hours?" Tiffany asked in horror. "I'm saving money for a new car, Aunt Rose. You can't do that."

Tracy beamed. "She won't have to. This hopefully solves our problem," she told them. "When everyone finds out Drew is now a suspect, people will come right back over to the flower shop. My reputation and name will be cleared, and things will go back to normal."

"I hope so," her aunt sighed. "This has been one of the most stressful weeks as a business owner and a concerned aunt. I've been really worried about you, Tracy."

Tracy gave her a big hug. "No need to worry," she murmured as she embraced her aunt. "Everything Is going to be okay."

Just then, a woman walked through the front door of the shop. Tracy squinted, instantly recognizing her. It was the elderly woman who had been rude to her at the market a few days prior; instead of a scowl, though, she had a polite smile on her face.

"I need a bouquet of yellow roses," she told them cheerfully as she approached the front counter. "Please and thank you."

Tracy peered at her curiously. "Nice to see you again," she said quietly. "I remember you from the market..."

The woman blinked. "Oh, yes, hello," she smiled weakly. "Lovely to see you, too."

Tracy looked into her eyes. "It's nice that you've come into our shop today," she said. "We haven't had a customer in nearly a week. It's been very difficult on us."

The woman nodded. "I can imagine," she replied, not catching on to what Tracy was alluding to. "Say, did you ladies hear about that nasty Drew Blackwood?" she asked in a gossipy tone. "He was from a poor family in Kentucky, or Ohio, or somewhere dreadful in the Midwest. The Hamptons took him under their wing, and what did he do? He murdered their daughter. Can you believe it? He killed Heather."

Aunt Rose went to the buckets of roses and selected twelve yellow ones, pursing her lips as she listened to the older woman.

"Where did you hear that?" Tiffany asked.

"My friend, Mildreth, is a librarian," she told them. "She called me and told me Drew was arrested at the library just a half hour ago. Can you believe it? I knew he always had it in him; you can't take a poor, ill-bred farm boy out of Illinois and expect him to fit in in civilized society. It just isn't done."

Tiffany raised an eyebrow. "I thought you said Mr. Blackwood was from Kentucky or Ohio?"

"Does it matter?" she countered as Aunt Rose handed her the freshly wrapped bouquet. "He was trash. That's a fact. Heather was a debutante and a socialite, and now, she's gone. It's a shame. Her poor parents; they are pillars of this community, and I know they are devastated."

Tracy narrowed her eyes. "What else do you know about Drew Blackwood?" she asked. "What else did your friend say?"

"She really couldn't say much," the woman shrugged. "At least, that's what she said. Anyway, thanks for the flowers, ladies. So glad you are all back in action. See you later."

Tracy watched as the woman left with her flowers in hand. She felt a knot in her stomach as she thought of Drew Blackwood's arrest; he had thought *she* was the killer, and as he was being arrested, he insisted he was innocent. Tracy felt torn. Had Drew Blackwood killed his wife, or was there still a murderer on the loose?

16

That evening, Tracy snuggled up on her couch, pulling Mr. Sydney into her lap. She kissed the top of his head, smiling as she felt his soft fur tickle her cheeks.

"You're going to have a dog sibling soon," she gushed as he rubbed his face on her neck. "What do you think about that? You've never met a dog before, Mr. Sydney."

Mr. Sydney's eyes widened; it was as if he knew exactly what she was saying. He flared his nostrils and let out an angry hiss, and Tracy bit her lip.

Her cell phone rang, and her heart raced when she realized it was Warren. She had been trying to give him his space; she knew he was terribly upset about his job, and she did not want to smother him when it was clear he needed to clear his head. Still, she was excited to see him calling, and she answered the phone on the second ring.

"Hey, you," she said. "How are you, Warren?"

"Hey," he greeted her, his voice flat. "Just wanted to check in."

She sighed. He didn't sound like his usual self, but she hoped talking with her would lift his spirits.

"I'm doing pretty well, honey," she told him as Mr. Sydney spun around in a circle and then settled in her lap. "There is some big news about the case."

"I heard," he replied curtly.

"They think Drew Blackwood killed his wife," she explained. "I don't know if I am a suspect anymore, but I feel pretty sure that things are gonna be okay for me and my name will officially be cleared soon. Isn't that great?"

She heard her fiancé exhale loudly. "It's fantastic," he wearily grunted.

"Babe," she murmured. "What's wrong?"

Warren took a deep breath. "I think you need to stop being so nosy," he told her. "You really like to poke your nose into other people's business, Tracy. This case isn't about you, it's about bringing Heather's murderer to justice. I think it's a little weird that you are so preoccupied about clearing your name when someone is *dead.*"

She felt as though he had slapped her in the face. "War-ren," she whimpered. "That seems a little harsh…."

"I'm sorry," he apologized. "Maybe I'm just envious that your problems are getting taken care of and I am still the loser who has been laid off."

"Babe," she started. "Your problems are my problems, and vice versa. We are partners. We are a couple. Just because my name is going to be cleared doesn't mean that I am any less worried about *you*. I've been worried to death about you, honey."

"Really?"

"Really. You're my fiancé, Warren. How could I not worry about you?"

Her heart pounded in her chest; she hoped he understood she loved him and was on his side.

"I know," he muttered. "I'm sorry I've been such a basket case, Tracy. You deserve better. I'm worried, though; this Heather Blackwood case feels a little fishy to me. I have a feeling it's more complicated than we even know. That's what happens when money and murder are thrown into the same situation."

Tracy felt a chill down her spine. Was that a coincidence, or was Warren right?"

"What do you want me to do?" she asked. "I can take care of myself, you know; I've been doing it for nearly forty years."

Warren scoffed. "Tracy, when it comes to murder and millionaires, no one can take care of themselves. This is way over your head, and I'm worried the Blackwoods and the Hamptons are more dangerous than we even know..."

She raised an eyebrow. "I guess we'll just agree to disagree," she said shortly. "I have to go. Talk to you later."

Before he could reply, she hung up the phone. Irritation flooded her chest; she knew she was a strong, independent woman, and she did not need her fiancé, or anyone else, to tell her what to do.

Her phone rang again. She did not want to talk to Warren; she was angry at the way he disregarded her strength and intelligence, and she needed some time to cool down.

The ringtone, however, was not the one she had assigned to Warren; she looked at her phone and realized it was Isabelle, one of her dearest friends, calling.

"Hey girl," she answered. "What's up?"

"Oh, thank goodness you answered," Isabelle breathed. "Tracy, where have you been? You haven't been answering any of my calls or texts."

"Sorry," she apologized, knowing she had ignored three

calls and nearly ten texts from her friend over the last week. "There is a lot going on right now."

"Such as?"

Tracy filled her in on the trouble in Fern Grove. "Ouch," Isabelle exclaimed when Tracy was finished. "That's awful, Tracy. I'm so sorry. What does Warren say about all of this?"

She felt her face darken. "Warren," she grumbled. "He hasn't had a lot to say. To be honest, I'm a little miffed right now. He seems to think I'm some ditzy damsel in distress, not a bright, hard-working, resourceful woman who has a college degree."

"What do you mean?" her friend asked. "Is he being over-bearing?"

"Not really," she admitted. "He just said some things that really got under my skin."

Isabelle giggled. "If you want to pull an Isabelle, I have an idea that could solve all of your problems."

"Oh, yeah?"

"Maybe it's time for new beginnings," she urged Tracy. "Maybe it's time you left all the endless drama in that beautiful but crazy town of yours and come back to the city."

Tracy scrunched her face as she considered Isabelle's words. "I love it here in Fern Grove. What would I be coming back to in Portland? CMB Capital? I know we had some great times while I worked there before I was part of the wave that was let go. You're forever reminding me of how things are so drab over there."

Isabelle cleared her throat. "Actually, I've left."

Tracy gasped.

"I left a few weeks ago," Isabelle continued. "I needed a fresh start. And, it sounds to me like you need a fresh start as well. What do you think?"

"But I thought things were taking a turn for the better at

CMB?" Tracy said as she moved her cell phone to her other ear.

"All good things must come to an end," Isabelle giggled. "I have a new job in banking at Wilson and Watson across town. It's a great firm, Tracy; it's owned by women, and they are committed to diversity and inclusion. It's a much better situation than we had before. I've told my boss and everyone in my department about you, and they can't wait to see you. If you apply, I can almost guarantee that the job will be yours. What do you say?"

Tracy blinked at her. "Wow! I don't know what to say…"

"You don't have to say anything… yet. I really wanted to call you and convince you to come join me at my new bank. What do you think? You can bring that big brain of yours back to the city and we can start fresh. What do you think? Come on, Tracy. Maybe this is the break you've been looking for."

"I don't know," she hung her head. "Maybe I should just get away for a night or two. Would you be open to hosting a guest? I think drinks and dinner and some girl time could help…"

"You think about it," Isabelle told her. "My door is always open for you. Let me know if you are coming, and I will start washing the sheets in the guest room and getting the house aired out."

They said goodbye, and Tracy held the phone to her chest. Maybe getting away from Fern Grove for a night was just what she needed. Perhaps running away to the city she had once loved and clearing her head would solve her problems.

Their conversation made Tracy think about her future; with Warren acting so off and things feeling so out of hand in Fern Grove, did she really want to stay in a small town for the rest of her life? She thought of her past life as a city girl, going out, working at the bank, and having a lifestyle most would be envious of.

Tracy fetched her laptop computer from her bedroom and opened it, searching for and clicking the link to the website for Wilson and Watson. On the career opportunities page, she saw there was a job opening. Tracy clicked the link, and the page revealed a job that was within her skill set and expertise.

Tracy adored her aunt and loved her job at the flower shop, but she could not explain what came over her in that moment; she opened the online application and began to fill it out, hitting send as soon as she finished.

"Maybe I'll have to change my own luck," she thought as she received an email confirming her submission. "Maybe it's time to get out of town for good."

After a fitful night of sleep, Tracy awoke abruptly as the sound of thunder filled her bedroom. She reached for Mr. Sydney, who was sleeping at her feet, and pulled him close to her. Lightening began to strike, and she could see the flashes of light cracking outside of her apartment as she peeked out the window.

Rain beat down on the roof of her apartment, and she worried that the weather was worsening as the heavy thudding of thunder roared through the town. Tracy reached for her phone and cringed; it was only six in the morning, but she knew she would never get back to sleep.

She had two missed calls from her aunt, and she quickly dialed her number.

"Good morning," she croaked into her cell phone.

"Well, good morning to you," her aunt replied. "I'm worried this town is going to flood, Tracy. I have never seen rain like this. I think we need to build an ark instead of arranging flowers today."

Tracy smiled. "I'll bring the hammer if you bring the nails."

Her aunt sighed. "I'm worried about the flower shop, Tracy," she shared, and Tracy noted the concern in her voice. "This weather is wicked; do you think I should have Tiffany come in or just tell her to stay home? I don't really think it's appropriate to ask anyone to be out in this kind of storm if they don't have to be…"

Tracy thought for a moment. "It's Thursday, right?"

"Yes, it is."

"Then you are in luck," she told her aunt. "Tiffany comes in at noon on Thursdays, remember? This storm will probably pass by the time she wakes up."

"Oh, thank goodness," Aunt Rose breathed in relief. "Okay. Well dear, you enjoy your day off, and I'll plan on seeing you in three days. I'm taking the weekend off, but I'll be back bright and early on Monday."

"Well…."

"Well?"

Tracy cleared her throat. "Isabelle called," she began. "I might go out of town for a few days."

"What? Tracy, you aren't supposed to leave town," her aunt reminded her.

"It's for something special," she told her aunt, trying her best to sound nonchalant. The truth was that she knew how persuasive her friend, Isabelle, could be and anticipated she would get a confirmation email about a job interview in the next few days.

"I might have a job interview in the city," she admitted quietly. "At Isabelle's new bank."

"What? You're leaving the flower shop?" Her aunt asked in shock.

"It's not set in stone," she assured her. "But I wanted to tell you."

"I think it's a horrible idea," her aunt frowned. "And besides, you can't leave Fern Grove. That's what the police said. This timing seems awful. What is wrong with In Season, anyway? We offer you so much autonomy and a wonderful work environment. Isn't that enough for you?"

"I don't know. Besides, they never charged me with anything, so legally, I don't think they can tell me what to do or not do."

Her aunt gulped. "I don't think it's a good idea," she warned her niece. "Think about this, Tracy: what if leaving town makes you look guilty?"

"Then it makes me look guilty," she replied sharply. "The people in this town were quick to judge me, so now, I just don't care what they think."

Aunt Rose exhaled. "I don't think it's a good idea," she repeated. "But I know you are going to do what you want. Just keep me posted as to what your plans are. I love you, Tracy. Your Uncle Frank would be so proud of you, and I know I am. You're a wonderful woman with loads of potential, and I can't wait to see how your life plays out."

Her heart softened at her aunt's loving words. "I love you, too."

"I'll always be here for you, Tracy. No matter what."

She hung up the phone, feeling a bit of guilt for the tone she had used to speak to her dear aunt. Why was she punishing Aunt Rose for her own frustrations? She needed to be nicer, and she decided to reset her bad attitude.

"What should I do to start this day over?" she asked Mr. Sydney. "I'm off to a grumpy start, and it isn't even seven in the morning yet."

She glanced over at the window. The rain was still coming down, but the thunder and lightning had stopped. Tracy rose from her bed to walk to the bathroom, but she stumbled on a pair of her athletic shoes that she had carelessly left by the side of her bed.

"Ouch," she moaned as she slammed her knee into her nightstand. "That's what I get for leaving my shoes out…"

Suddenly, she had an idea. Tracy knew she needed to get into a better mood, and what better way than to exercise? She hastily tore off her pajamas and changed into a pair of running tights and a long-sleeve t-shirt, put a baseball cap on over her dirty hair, and added a pair of gloves.

"I'm the type of woman who starts her days with a workout," she decided, happy to be taking charge of something. "Mr. Sydney, I'll be back soon."

Tracy left the apartment and took off on a jog. The wind was rough, and the rain stung her face, but she enjoyed the wholesome ache in her legs and she picked up each foot and moved her body. Tracy had never been much of an athlete, but today, she felt strong and fierce as she ran through the dark, cold, rainy morning.

She headed over to the beach, enjoying the thunderous crashes of dark ocean water on the shore. She had always preferred the pool over the beach, but this morning, there was something magical about the way the dark, wet sand clung to her sneakers and the thick clouds tore through the sky as though they were racing each other.

She inhaled the smell of rain, fish, and salt water. Tracy loved the fresh air in Fern Grove; it was one of the things she adored most about small town life, and she was always eager to catch a whiff of the salty air each time she stepped outdoors.

As she navigated the thick, sticky sand, she noticed a dark figure in the distance. Knowing her cell phone and a little bottle of pepper spray were tucked into her back pocket, she continued her jog, feeling safe, though cautious, as she ran along the beach.

When she neared the figure, her heart dropped. It was Drew Blackwood. Dressed in a black athletic jacket and matching sweatpants, he was skipping rocks along the shoreline. She felt a cold sweat on her body, and she turned on her heel, eager to avoid an interaction with him. Before she could dart away, though, she heard him call out her name.

"Tracy Adams," he shouted, and reluctantly, she turned around. He walked up to her, a stern look on his face.

"Hey," she greeted him, taking a step back and away. "Can I help you?"

He crossed his arms over his chest. "Yeah, you can," he told her gruffly, his eyebrows knitting together into a deep frown. "I need answers about what happened to Heather."

She stared at him. "I don't know what happened to Heather," she told him. "Aren't you supposed to be in jail? Why are you here?"

"They didn't have enough evidence," he shrugged. "They couldn't prove that I murdered Heather. They let me out without charging me, which is what I heard they did to *you*."

She looked into his eyes. "I didn't kill her," she whispered. "I swear on my aunt's life, my fiancé's life, and my life. I didn't do it."

He sighed. "Let's walk," he said quietly.

"I don't want to go with you," she refused. "I don't know you or trust you; what if you try to hurt me?"

He pointed over at the security cameras positioned atop the old lifeguard stand. "You think I would be stupid enough to do anything to anyone while on camera? Please."

He started walking down the beach. Tracy was filled with questions and curiosity, and against her better judgement, she followed him.

"I heard you knew her," he murmured as the rain poured down. "Heather."

"A long time ago," she corrected him. "Back in high school."

"She was such a beauty back then," he noted. "Well, she was when I met her in college, a few years later."

Tracy thought of Heather's perfect skin and clothes when she had walked into the flower shop. "She still looked like a model before she died," she added, and Drew nodded.

"Heather was a force of nature," he began. "She wanted what she wanted, and she would have done anything to get her way. She had a lot of enemies, you know. I thought you were one of them, but now, after talking to you, I think you were just an innocent bystander who got caught up in this mess."

"Tell me about Heather's enemies," she asked softly. "Why did people hate her?"

He stopped and turned to look directly into her eyes. "Heather did what she wanted. She did as she pleased," he explained matter-of-factly. "In the business world, old, educated, powerful men did not take well to a young, beautiful, brilliant woman coming into their game and beating them time and time again."

"Who were her enemies? Who specifically?"

"Where could I start?" he laughed. "Let's just say Heather was a rising real estate mogul and had a promising career in politics. Try to imagine the types of people who dominate those fields and then try to imagine how much they *hated* having Heather as a force against them..."

She bit her lip. "It sounds like she was mixed up with some scary people."

He chuckled. "That's the understatement of the century... between her real estate gigs and political career, she had a lot of competition, and a lot of enemies."

Tracy decided to change the subject. "What about you?" she asked him. "What are you gonna do now? Are you close with your in-laws?"

He scowled. "I was never good enough for them," he

muttered. "I'm getting out of the Pacific Northwest," he declared. "I'm going back to the Midwest; there is a coaching position that opened up at Indiana University, and I want it. I'm going back to my roots and getting out of here."

"That sounds nice," she told him. "Sometimes, getting back to our roots can be the best thing for us. I bet Heather would be really happy for you."

He shot her a look. "Heather didn't care what I did," he sighed. "For her, I was an accessory. Heather was the rich girl with the big heart who rescued the handsome scholarship kid and married him. I was nothing to her, and nothing to her parents. I want to go somewhere where I can be a some-body to someone."

She stopped, looking over at his face. "Did you do it?" she asked softly. "Kill Heather? So you could start over in Indiana?"

He shook his head. "I couldn't kill a fly."

"Did you help someone kill her? Tell me, Drew. Did you set her up? Did you set *me* up? Did *you* call the flower shop and send me over to Marshall Street?"

He gave her a hateful look. "You don't know what you're talking about," he hissed as he turned on his heel and walked away from her.

She stared at him as he left, wondering if she was looking at an innocent widower or a conniving killer. Tracy did not know the answer, but she was determined to find out what was going on.

Aunt Rose waved her cell phone in the air. "I have three thousand friends," she squealed, her eyes bright with excitement.

It was early the next morning, and she, Tracy, and Tiffany had just opened the flower shop. They were off to a slow start, but the sun was shining, and the three women were in better spirits. Tiffany had asked Aunt Rose about how her social media efforts were going, and Aunt Rose was regaling them with tales of her newfound friends and the connections they had made.

"A thousand friends?" Tiffany gasped in awe. "You're practically a celebrity; you should start an Instagram account."

Aunt Rose shook her head. "I want to stick with one platform," she said firmly. "Besides, I get a hundred friend requests each day; can you imagine how many friends I am gonna make in the next few weeks? I won't have time for any other social media, Tiffany."

Tracy grabbed Aunt Rose's phone out of her hand. "Let

me see this," she muttered to herself as she pulled up her aunt's home page on Facebook.

She gasped. The page was loaded with personal information about her aunt; she had added her home address and her phone number, and in a picture where she posed with her car, her treasured vintage Mercedes, the license plate could be seen.

"Aunt Rose," she chided her. "What did I tell you about internet safety? You have thrown all of this personal information out into the world, and anyone can snatch it; what if this falls into the wrong hands and something happens?"

Her aunt laughed. "Tracy, please; the only people who can see my information are my friends."

"Do you know every single one of your Facebook friends personally? *No.* They shouldn't all have access to your personal information," she declared, holding her head high.

Aunt Rose grabbed at the cell phone. "Give it back," she insisted. "Tracy, that's *my* phone. I am a grown woman. Show me some respect."

The phone buzzed and Tracy looked down at the screen. It was a text message from someone called Simon.

"Who is Simon?" she asked her aunt.

Aunt Rose's face turned the exact color of a tomato. "What? Who? It must be a mistake."

Tracy raised an eyebrow. "A mistake, huh? Aunt Rose, how could someone's information mistakenly find its way to your phone?"

Her aunt scowled. "If you must know," she began, clearly flustered. "Simon is a lovely gentleman I met on Facebook. He lives in a darling little house in the Cotswolds."

"The Cotswolds?" Tiffany asked. "Is that the new apartment complex down the street?"

Rose laughed. "No, silly," she corrected the young woman.

"The Cotswolds is a region in England. It's a lovely area filled with stone houses and green fields."

Tracy's eyes widened. "Wait a second," she halted. "You're chatting online with someone you met on Facebook? He lives in England? Is this really a good idea?"

Her Aunt scowled. "It's none of your business, Tracy," she repeated. "I think we need to change the subject."

"I think that's a good idea," Tiffany added cautiously.

Aunt Rose pasted a smile on her face. "So, Tracy," she began. "Any news about the case?"

Tracy sighed. "Not really," she admitted. "I haven't heard any updates. Besides running into Drew Blackwood on the beach, there's nothing new."

Tiffany blinked. "What about the house?" she asked. "The Marshall Street house. Did you ever find out who lives there? Or... *lived* there?"

Tracy shrugged. "My research mission at the library was foiled by Drew's arrest, remember?"

Aunt Rose patted her shoulder. "Don't worry too much," she urged her niece. "You're innocent, and we know that. This will all quiet down sooner than later, dear. I promise."

Just then, the front door of the flower shop opened and a man dressed in a tailored blue pinstripe suit sauntered in. He was handsome, with a flash of gray hair around his temples and a distinguished presence.

"Can I help you?" her aunt asked. "Looking for flowers for someone special?"

He shook his head and looked straight at Tracy. "Do you deliver to corporate functions?"

She was taken aback by his question. "What? Like events? Yes, we do; we have limited delivery services, but for a fee, we are able to deliver arrangements to events."

He leaned in. "Excellent."

Tiffany narrowed her eyes. "What kind of event, sir?"

He gave her a side-eye smile. "Oh, you know, just a business thing."

Aunt Rose nodded at him. "Are you thinking about large table arrangements, or general decor pieces? Can you tell me about your budget and goals of the event? I always like a holistic view of the situation before I start creating arrangements; it helps me to keep things aligned with what my customers truly want."

He frowned. "So you deliver flowers and you can create table arrangements *and* general decor?"

"And pieces to decorate food and beverage tables, and garlands, and pretty much any sort of item you can think of," Tiffany boasted, her eyes sparkling. "If you can dream it, we can do it. Rose is a wizard when it comes to creating gorgeous florals."

Aunt Rose shook her head. "You flatter me, Tiffany," she chuckled before turning back to the man. "What kind of event is it? How many guests are you expecting?"

He said nothing but reached for one of the many In Season business cards that was displayed on the front counter. "I'll take one of these."

Tracy waved at him awkwardly. "So... should we start an order for you?"

He shook his head. "Not today." Turning on his heel, he left in silence, all three women staring after him.

Tracy stared at her aunt. "What *was* that?" she asked. "Or better yet... who was that? Was that weird to you guys?"

"He gave me the creeps," Tiffany chimed in. "He looked like a creepy old rich man. Did you see the way he was staring at you, Tracy? Maybe he liked you or something."

"Weird," Tracy muttered as she tucked a loose tendril of hair behind her ear. "He seemed fishy to me too, Tiffany."

"Creepy, but handsome," Tiffany added. "Like in a George

Clooney way. Or a Brad Pitt way. Older and intense, but very handsome."

Tracy watched outside as he crossed the street. Who was the older man in the suit? Was he a future customer for In Season? Tracy did not know, but she had a weird feeling in her stomach. Despite the sun shining outside, a welcome departure from the recent awful weather, she could not shake the feeling that the man had come to the shop for more than just a business card.

Aunt Rose's phone rang and Tracy winced as she heard the ringtone: it was a song with immature, childish lyrics, and she gasped as the singer made a sound that sounded like flatulence.

"Aunt Rose!"

Her aunt looked apologetic. "I don't know how to change it," she whispered before answering the phone call.

Tiffany looked at Tracy. "I don't think Rose was destined for a smartphone," she laughed, though Tracy did not think it was very funny that her Aunt had accidentally downloaded a rude song as her ringtone.

"This is Rose," her aunt answered in a warm tone. "Yes? Yes. No? Well, I just…"

Tracy could hear a loud voice coming from the other end of the phone. "Who is it?" she mouthed to her aunt.

"Next Move," Aunt Rose mouthed back, and Tracy's stomach churned.

"Okay," Rose replied to the caller. "Yes, we can manage. I understand."

She ended the call, and Tracy noticed the worry that had flooded her face. "What was that about?"

Her aunt wrinkled her nose. "I called earlier about the call logs," she explained to them, her eyes wide. "They said they would call me back, which is why I just took their call. The caller was awful, though; it was a man, and he told me he has better things to do than check a phone log and that I need to stop bothering them, or I would be sorry."

Tracy bit her lip. "Did he give his name?"

"No," Aunt Rose shrugged. "He just said he was from Next Move."

"Can I see your phone?" Tiffany asked, extending her hand with her palm facing up. "I want to see the phone number."

Rose gave the phone to Tiffany, who gasped as she looked down at the screen. "The call was from a blocked number," she whispered.

"That's it," Tracy told them. "I'm going over to Next Move and talking to them myself. We aren't going to sit around and let this go any farther."

Fifteen minutes later, Tracy arrived at Next Move's Fern Grove location. It was a sleek, modern building, with an industrial aesthetic and floor to ceiling windows. Tracy took a long breath as she stood outside and then marched into the lobby.

A thin raven-haired receptionist seated at a round desk intercepted her. "Can I help you?"

"I need some answers," Tracy told her, glancing around at the empty lobby. "I'm Tracy Adams. I work at In Season, my aunt's flower shop. We just received a threatening phone call that was supposedly from someone here at Next Move, and I want some information."

The receptionist smiled at her. "Oh, In Season, of course. Can I see some ID? If you can show me some ID, Ms. Adams,

I can access our records and find out who has called you from Next Move."

Tracy stared at her. "I don't have my ID," she stammered. "I mean, I do, but I didn't bring it with me...."

The receptionist made a face. "I'm so sorry, but I can't help you. Please come back when you have your identification and I can assist you in any way you need, Ms. Adams."

"Please," she pleaded, placing her hands on the round desk and staring at the receptionist. "I *need* your help. Someone just threatened my aunt and said they called from Next Move. I need to know what's going on."

The receptionist gave her a sympathetic look. "It sounds quite frustrating," she agreed. "But our company policy requires visitors to provide identification. I don't make the rules, Ms. Adams, but I must enforce them."

Tracy furrowed her brow. "Fine," she exhaled as she lifted her hands and looked around, spotting a black metal staircase in the center of the room. "If you can't help me, I'll have to help myself."

The receptionist stood up. "I suggest you go," she said firmly, seeing Tracy's eyes on the staircase. "Do not take a step farther into the office, ma'am."

"I want to speak with your manager," Tracy insisted. "Who is your boss? I want to speak with her *now*."

"Hey."

They both turned as an older man in a gray suit walked down the stairs. "I'm Alex Hunt, the managing partner here at Next Move's Fern Grove office. Can I help you, Ma'am?"

The receptionist breathed a sigh of relief. "Yes, Mr. Hunt, can you please assist this woman?"

Tracy stared at him. "I need to see your call logs," she insisted. "Someone from Next Move just called my aunt and threatened her."

His green eyes filled with alarm. "What? Is this a joke? Who is your Aunt?"

"Rose Bishop from In Season, the flower shop," she explained. "I'm Tracy, her niece. We have a partnership with Next Move."

He nodded vigorously. "Of course, you do," he agreed. "I signed the documents agreeing to the deal. What's this about a threatening call? I don't understand…"

She held up Rose's cell phone, which she had brought with her to the office. "Someone called my aunt and made threats," she told him. "They said they were from Next Move. We checked the number, and the call was from a blocked number. I want to see your call logs and try to find out who called my aunt and why."

He took a deep breath and ran his hands through his silver hair. "I'm sorry this happened," he told her. "Come to my office; we can access the records together."

"Mr. Hunt," the receptionist stopped him. "Don't you need her identification?"

He shot her a look. "It's fine," he sighed. "Come on, Ms. Adams. We can speak more in my office."

He led her upstairs to his office, a large space filled with leather furniture and a huge conference table in the center of the room. Photographs of Mr. Hunt and a woman, presumably his wife, filled a shelf in the corner, and there was a tall house plant by the window.

"Have a seat," he urged her, pointing to a large brown leather chair in front of his desk. "Please make yourself comfortable."

She sat down, and he went to his desk and started typing frantically on his computer. He clicked a button, and a pile of papers began to print from a machine beneath his desk. He gathered the papers and glanced at them and pulled a highlighter out of his desk drawer. He made a few circles on the papers, and then handed them to Tracy.

"These are our logs from the last month," he explained. "The circled numbers are the calls to In Season, along with the name of the caller, the call details, and any orders made during the call."

She scanned the first column and saw several calls she recognized: several orders from Next Move, conversations to discuss adjustments to the delivery schedule, and a brainstorming session with the Next Move marketing team to decide on some color schemes for a new subdivision on Laurel Avenue.

"I know these calls," she told him.

"That's what I thought," he frowned. "Our official records don't show *any* calls from today, Ms. Adams."

She pursed her lips. "And they don't show any calls from the day Heather Blackwood died..."

His head jerked up. "Did you know Heather?"

She shrugged. "We went to high school together. I didn't know her well."

He looked down at the floor. "I've known... knew... Heather since she was a baby," he informed her. "Her father and I were business partners; we started Next Move from the ground up."

"I didn't know that," she offered. "So you knew the family well?"

"Yes," he shared. "They were like family to me; her father was my best friend. He passed away a year ago, and not a day goes by that I don't wish he and I were out on the golf course, working on a deal, or sharing a beer on a nice day."

She nodded. "I'm sorry for your losses," she whispered. "Of your best friend, and now, Heather."

"She was like a daughter to me," he mentioned, resting his chin in his hand. "It's been so complicated since she passed."

Her eyes met his. "Complicated?"

"Her shares of the business were transferred upon her death," he stated. "I now share a business with someone I barely know. It's odd…"

"Who is the other owner?" she asked, leaning forward in her chair.

His face darkened. "Drew Blackwood," he muttered. "He is the majority owner and stockholder, now. It's a mess."

Confusion flooded her mind. Drew Blackwood owned Next Move? She started to think back to their conversation on the beach; he had not mentioned this development as he shared his plans to move to Indiana. What was going on?

Alex Hunt rose to his feet. "I've clearly babbled too much," he chuckled politely. "I should get back to work. Sorry about the calls, Ms. Adams. Perhaps someone is simply pulling a rude prank."

"Maybe," she agreed half-heartedly. "I hope so."

As Tracy left Next Move, she wandered over to Marshall Street. She did not know why she was going there, but felt as though visiting the house where Heather had been found would give her some clarity.

She stood across the street from 111 Marshall Street, feeling her heart pounding in her chest. Who had called Aunt Rose? Who had killed Heather Blackwood? Would her name ever truly be cleared? As she weighed these questions, she did not hear the heavy sound of footsteps approaching her, and she nearly jumped out of her skin when she felt someone tap on her shoulder.

She let out a screech, turning to find the man who had come into the flower shop for a business card, staring at her.

"What are you doing?" she cried, holding her hand to her heart and feeling it race. "Why did you sneak up on me like that?"

He smirked at her. "Sean Barnes," he said, holding out his

hand. "I realized I didn't properly introduce myself the other day.

"Tracy Adams," she replied curtly. "Can I help you?"

He shook his head. "I saw you over here and had to say hello. I really wanted to get your number the other day, but I lost my nerve…"

She held up her left and flashed her engagement ring at him. "Sorry."

He laughed. "Forgive me," he smiled kindly. "I should have known a gorgeous woman like you had someone waiting on her. Well, you can't blame me for trying."

She blushed, feeling pleased at the compliment in spite of herself, and then raised an eyebrow. "Why are you out here staring at these houses?"

"I could ask you the same thing."

She put her hands on her hips. "Well?"

"Well? The truth is, I'm a hustler, Tracy. I'm trying to hustle my way into becoming the top realtor in town. My boutique real estate company is successful, but I want to have a company like Next Move. I'm not at that level yet, but I will be. Soon. Someday, I'll sell these fancy houses, and maybe even have a company of my own."

She stared at him. "You came out here to stare at houses you want to sell?"

"It's called manifesting my fortune," he corrected her. "Maybe it's a little hippie dippie, but it works for me. This is something I did when I broke into the restaurant industry back in 2009, and I know it works."

"You had a restaurant?"

"Five," he told her. "I'm a hustler. I make moves and I don't settle for less than my potential."

She noted the earnest expression on his face. "You once worked for Next Move, huh?"

He cocked his head to the side. "Once upon a time. They

take their customers and vendors for granted; I used to work there, and all sorts of weird things went on behind the scenes."

"Weird things?"

He shook his head. "Well, not weird, per se. Just awkward. There was a lot of nepotism, and if the Hamptons didn't like you, or the vendors you supplied, you were out. That's how I lost my job. Old Howard Hampton didn't like a referral I made to a furniture company, and I was out. He hired his own son to replace me...a son who had no experience in the business. That's a typical Hampton move, though."

She could see the anger on his face. "It sounds like you had a bad experience with them," she commented quietly.

"You think?" he replied sarcastically. "It's all over now, though; Heather is dead, and I heard her husband inherited her shares. I'm sure he'll sell them off sooner than later, and that company will no longer be run by Hamptons. It's about time, I say…"

He looked at her. "That flower shop of yours is nice. Maybe someday, I'll partner with you and your aunt to design arrangements for the houses *I* am selling."

"We'll see," she told him.

He gave her a little wave. "Well, it's been a pleasure, Tracy Adams. A real pleasure…"

She watched as he made his way down the block. Sean Barnes clearly loved the real estate business, but she had been stricken by some of his comments about the Hamptons and Next Move. He seemed to really despise them.

Sean turned a corner and disappeared from view. Tracy felt a pit in her stomach. Was Sean just an ordinary real estate agent in the making, or did he have it out for the Hampton family in a dangerous way?

Tracy headed back to In Season and was excited to find the shop brimming with customers upon her return. She could barely make it in the door; people were standing shoulder to shoulder in front of the counter, and she flashed her aunt a huge smile when she made it over to her.

"This is great," she exclaimed as they looked out into the busy room.

"Can you believe it? We are back," her aunt declared. "I want to hear about your visit to Next Move, but let's chat later? We have some big orders to fill, my dear!"

At the end of the day, they closed the flower shop and counted the funds in the cash register, thrilled to find they had made a major profit. "This is the best day of business we've had in a month," Rose announced. "Well done, ladies."

Tiffany clapped her hands together. "We are back on top."

Aunt Rose turned to look at Tracy. "Any news from Next Move?"

Tracy shook her head. "No, not really. I'm too tired to talk about it, to be honest; it's been a long day…."

Aunt Rose hugged her. "That's fine," she promised. "The call didn't scare me. We will just pretend like it never happened."

She dismissed them, and Tracy went home, eager for a soak in her bathtub and some snuggles with Mr. Sydney. As she approached her apartment, she saw Warren waiting outside, a bouquet of red roses in his hands.

"Honey?"

He grinned at her. "That waiter dropped the charges," he shared. "I'm back, Tracy. I'm a police officer again."

She dashed to him and threw herself into his arms. "I am so happy for you," she whispered into his ear as he held her tight. "Oh, Warren, this is such good news."

He set her back down on the ground and gave her a long kiss on the lips. "I'm sorry I was so crazy when I was on leave," he apologized, his face drawn. "I didn't act like the man I am or the man you deserve."

"You were in a dark place," she shrugged. "Though if it happens again, I want you to promise you will talk to a therapist, okay? I don't want you to stay stuck in depression when there is help available."

"Deal," he swore. "Though I hope to never be in this position again."

She invited him into her apartment, and he sat down on her green couch. Mr. Sydney came over and rubbed his face on Warren's legs. "Awww, the cat is happy for you," she commented as she sat down next to her fiancé and rested her head on his shoulder. "I'm glad you're back, babe."

"Me too," he beamed, but then his face turned dark. "Did you hear the news?"

The color drained from her face. "What? What news?"

"About the Blackwood murder?"

"No," she told him. "I've honestly been staying away from the newspaper and television; with so much gossip and trouble from the media these days, I want to stay *out* of it."

He stared into her eyes. "This isn't good," he muttered. "It's Drew. Drew Blackwood. He's missing, Tracy. We think he's left town."

Her eyes widened. "Does that mean what I think it does?"

He nodded. "That Drew Blackwood killed his wife and skipped town? Yes, honey. That's what it looks like, and I promise you I am going to work around the clock to find him, bring him to justice, and formally clear your name."

The next day, Tracy made her way to Aunt Rose's house; her aunt had invited her over for a girls' day on their day off, and she was excited for some time to relax and unwind.

"There's my favorite niece," she greeted Tracy as she walked in the front door.

Tracy laughed. "You mean your only niece," she corrected, but she hugged her aunt and gave her a kiss on the cheek. "What should we do today?" she asked as she sat down on her Aunt's rattan chair.

"I was thinking a movie sounded nice," her aunt replied.

"Do you have something in mind?"

Before Aunt Rose could answer, her phone started making little beeps. "You changed your ring tone," she observed as Aunt Rose reached for her cell phone.

"I figured out how to remove that nasty song," she proudly told her niece. "I added these cute little beeps as my text tones. They tell me when someone has texted me."

"I know what a text tone is," Tracy laughed. "Who texted you?"

"Oh, no one," her aunt replied coyly, and Tracy peered over to try to see whose name was on the screen.

"Don't be nosy," she chided Tracy, and they settled in to watch Legally Blonde, Tracy's favorite movie.

Five minutes into the film, however, Rose's phone began

to beep again. She picked it up, typed a message, and moments later, another series of beeps. This continued for twenty-five minutes until Tracy lost her patience.

"That sound is driving me nuts," she told her aunt. "Can you silence your phone? Please?"

Aunt Rose shrugged. "I don't know how."

She handed the phone to Tracy, and Tracy pushed the volume button. "There. Now it won't make noise."

Before she could give the cell phone back, there was a knock at the front door. Aunt Rose got up and answered it, and then returned to the living room. "Tracy, my neighbor, Mr. Jenkins, fell and needs a little help," she explained. "His wife just popped over. She needs me to help lift him; he's a large, elderly man, and they need another pair of hands."

Tracy nodded and rose to her feet. "Do you need my help?"

"No, just stay put," her aunt urged her. "I'll be back in five minutes. Just enjoy the movie, dear."

Aunt Rose rushed out of the house. Tracy glanced down at the cell phone, which was still in her hands. The screen lit up, and she finally opened the home screen and stared at the texts. They weren't texts at all, but rather messages through WhatsApp, a free online messaging program. She wrinkled her nose. Her aunt was having a long conversation with someone online, and though she knew it was wrong, she began to scroll through the messages.

The messages spanned back to the day Heather died, and it appeared that the person her aunt was chatting with was an older man. "I wonder if this is the guy who supposedly lives in England?" she thought as she returned to the most recent messages. She noticed the sender had removed their profile picture, and she saw that Aunt Rose did not have one, either.

A new message appeared on the screen:

Urgent. Danger ahead. Please watch out.

Tracy's body grew cold. What was going on? Who was her aunt talking to? She hastily composed a message and then sent it.

I got a new phone. Text me at 206-243-5335.

She closed her aunt's phone and waited. Ten seconds later, a text appeared on *her* cell phone.

Be careful, Rose. Danger.

"Danger?" she worried as she read and reread the message. What was going on? Was this the person who had been calling them and the caller who had sent them over to the Marshall House? Tracy's stomach churned. She didn't know what was going on, but she knew she *needed* to find out quickly, especially if someone was warning her aunt of impending *danger*.

The next morning, Tracy felt uneasy as she arrived at work. She had not known what to say to her aunt when she had returned to the house from helping her neighbor; she felt shame that she had broken a boundary and gone through her aunt's phone, but she also was genuinely concerned about whom her aunt was texting. What was going on? The mystery messenger had not messaged her again on her own cell phone, and Tracy was worried they had told Aunt Rose about the phone number switch.

When she saw her aunt, she felt relief as Rose walked over to hug her as though everything was normal. "Good morning, sunshine," Rose greeted her cheerfully. "Let's have a lovely day."

The morning was busy, but there was a slight lull in the afternoon. Aunt Rose walked over, locked the front door, and leaned against it, a smile on her face.

"We are *busy*," she commented as she fanned her face. "I need a little break. Did you two bring your lunches?"

Tiffany and Tracy nodded.

"Good. Let's sit down for twenty minutes or so and relax; we certainly earned the rest."

A few minutes later, the three women were leaning against the front counter, each with her lunch in front of her. Tiffany had an almond butter and jelly sandwich, Aunt Rose had a ham and cheese croissant, and Tracy was enjoying a tomato mozzarella salad.

Tiffany swallowed a bite of her sandwich and peered over at Tracy. "Any news on the case?"

Tracy frowned. "I wish people would stop asking me that," she said primly. "But as a matter of fact, yes. There is some news. Drew Blackwood has gone missing."

"Missing?" Aunt Rose cried. "Heather's husband? Does that mean…."

Tracy nodded. "It sounds like he's guilty," she explained, shrugging her shoulders. "You can't just leave town after something like this."

Her aunt shot her a look. "I remember someone talking about getting out of town to see Isabelle…"

Tracy blinked. "That's different," she countered. "Drew hasn't been heard from or seen. His cell phone is off, and his credit cards and wallet were found in his home. It's like he vanished off the face of the Earth. At least, that's what Warren told me."

"How is he doing?" Tiffany asked. "Is he happy to be back on the job?"

"So happy," she smiled. "That man was made to work; I don't think he's ever been so grateful for a ten-hour shift in all of his life."

They continued to chat until a hard knock came from the front door. Tracy nearly jumped out of her seat, feeling shocked by the loud noise, but she looked over to see Pastor Butler waving at them.

"I'll let him in," Tiffany told them as she got up and went to unlock the front door.

Pastor Butler stepped inside of the flower shop. "Good afternoon, ladies," he greeted them, his mustache twitching upward as he smiled at them. "How is everyone today?"

"We were just getting the updates on the Blackwood case from Tracy," Tiffany informed him, and he frowned.

"I can't believe Drew has gone missing," he muttered, hanging his head. "I hope nothing has happened to him."

"What do you mean?" Tracy asked. "It sounds like he's guilty and skipped town..."

Pastor Butler raised an eyebrow. "Drew is a good man," he protested. "It's a shame he's been wrapped up in all of this..."

The Pastor turned and looked at Aunt Rose. "Are you okay, Rose?" he asked. Her face was pinched and her eyes were filled with worry. She held her cell phone in front of her face.

"I'm fine," she answered weakly. "I just am a little worried about a friend of mine."

Pastor Butler nodded. "Who? Which friend? Someone I know, Rose?"

She shook her head. "No," she began. "It's someone I met on Facebook. We were talking a lot on a different app called WhatsApp, but for some reason, he's stopped responding to me."

Pastor Butler chuckled. "I am amazed by how many ways there are to communicate these days," he told them. "I don't have any sort of internet messaging, but I wish I knew more. These newfangled programs are too much for an old geezer like me. I'm sorry about your friend though, Rose. It's hard when we lose touch with our friends."

Tracy willed herself to smile; she wanted to confess to what she had done on her aunt's cell phone, but she was too scared to admit she had intervened with the WhatsApp messages.

"My friend was so nice to me," her aunt shared with the group. "Ever since my husband died, I've felt so lonely. Having someone to chat with was such a nice feeling, and he even made me feel like a beautiful, desired woman. I haven't felt like that in years: beautiful, worthy of affection, or wanted. It was nice."

Tracy's heart broke for her aunt. She didn't realize how difficult it had been for Aunt Rose when her uncle died; Rose was so brave and strong, and she rarely let herself show her vulnerabilities.

"I didn't know you felt that way," she murmured as she wrapped her arm around her aunt's shoulder. "I wish you had told me."

Her aunt sighed. "No one wants to listen to a sad, lonely widow," she lamented, her shoulders dropping. "I don't ever want to burden anyone with my problems."

"Aunt Rose, you are not a burden," she insisted, taking her aunt's hand and giving it a squeeze. "We are so lucky to have you."

They hugged again, and Tracy had an idea. "I'll be right back," she told them, scurrying off to the bathroom.

"I'm off, Tracy," Pastor Butler waved as she left the room. "Have a blessed day."

She locked the door behind her and pulled out her cell phone, opening up her text messages. She found the message she had sent to the mystery person and began to type.

Haven't heard from you. I hope all is well. I miss you.

She felt her hands shake as she sent the message, and then an instant later, her phone vibrated.

We should meet up.

Her eyes widened. What was she going to do? She bit her lip, and then sent her reply.

Let's meet at Grind it Out.

There was a pause, and then, a response.

Why don't we meet somewhere more private? Come to 24 Marshall Street at 9. I'll be waiting for you.

Her jaw dropped. The mysterious person behind the text messages had invited her to Marshall Street, the same street where Heather Blackwood had been murdered. Was there a connection? Tracy felt a knot in her stomach. What if the person who had been communicating with her aunt was the same person who lured her to the house where Heather had been found? She gulped and then replied to the message.

I'll be there.

22

"It's dead, Tracy."

She glared at Warren as they sat together on her couch. "I don't think it is."

"It's a dead end," he insisted, running a hand through his hair. "Tracy, I think your aunt has an admirer, and I think you've officially messed things up for her. I cannot believe you read through her messages and intervened like this."

She had hastily called Warren and asked him to come over as soon as her shift was through. He had brought pizza and soda with him, but it had gone untouched; once they started talking about the case, they started fighting about the messages.

"She's a grown woman," he told her. "You really stepped out of line, Tracy."

She felt frustration; didn't Warren know her aunt was older, naïve, and alone in the world? "I was just trying to help," she explained, her nostrils flaring as her anger intensified. "Why are you making me the bad guy?"

He rose to his feet. "I need to go," he sighed. "I'll make sure there are officers in the area. Tracy, I feel really uncomfortable with you going to an empty house to meet a stranger. I wish you would give it up and let this one go."

She said nothing, and he shook his head. "Suit yourself," he muttered as he left, slamming the door behind him.

Ten minutes later, she left her apartment. As Tracy walked to the Marshall Street, she felt her cell phone buzz, and she pulled it out of her pocket and found a text message from the mystery messenger.

Running a little late. Key is under the mat. Let yourself in and help yourself to anything in the fridge. Wine cellar is in the basement and you are welcome to help yourself to a glass of cabernet (or anything else). I'll be there soon. Watch for my black car.

Tracy let herself into the house, nervous as she stepped inside. The house was silent, and she was reminded of a few days earlier when she had been at the house where Heather was found.

She hung up her coat on the coat rack and made her way into the kitchen. There was a potted succulent hanging above the sink that looked a little dry, and she found an empty glass and filled it with cool water, giving the plant a drink.

After watering the plant, she went to the refrigerator and grabbed a bottle of water. She felt nervous. Who was going to be arriving at the house? Should she have brought something to protect herself? What if this was all an innocent rendezvous, and she prevented her aunt from meeting up with her paramour?

Tracy walked into the sitting room and stared at the window, her heart racing as a black car pulled up in front of the house. She craned her neck to see who was in the driver's seat, and she gasped as the driver got out of the car and approached the house.

"Sean Barnes?" she exclaimed as he sauntered up to the

front door. She felt adrenaline fill her body; it had been Sean all along. She remembered their conversation about the Hampton family; he had sounded so spiteful, and she was not surprised that he had killed Heather. She wondered why he had involved herself and Aunt Rose, but then realized he must have *hated* them for doing business with Next Move. It all made sense now. He had lured Tracy to the first house at Marshall Street to frame her, and now, he was planning to kill her aunt.

"But that's not gonna happen," she muttered as he walked into the house and came face to face with her.

"You? What are you doing here?"

She glared at him. "I know what you did," she glowered as she balled her hands into fists. "And I'm not going to let you hurt my family like you hurt Heather Blackwood."

"You shouldn't be here," he frowned as he took a step forward, but before he could reach Tracy, she turned on her heel and took off running.

"Where are you going?" he shouted as she ducked behind a sofa. "Come back here. You should not be inside of this house."

She leaped to her feet and ran upstairs, locking a door behind her.

"Come out right now," he warned her. "Or you'll be sorry!"

She was quiet for several minutes, and eventually, she heard the front door close. She peeked out the window of the bedroom where she was hiding and saw him get into his black car and drive away.

Tracy let out a sigh of relief as she pulled her cell phone and dialed her fiancé.

"Warren," she said breathlessly. "I know who did it."

"What? Are you okay?"

She exhaled. "It was Sean Barnes. That weird real estate

guy I told you about. Look, you have to come to the house; I'll explain everything."

"Is he still there?"

She shook her head as she made her way out of the bedroom and back downstairs. "He's gone," she told him. "He just left."

"Stay where you are," he told her, but before she could say goodbye, she heard footsteps in the house.

She quietly set the phone down at her feet and looked around. There was no one in the room, and she decided it was time she got out of the house; she was spooked enough for one day.

"Ms. Adams."

She turned around to see Alex Hunt from Next Move walking down the stairs.

"Oh, thank goodness you are here," she cried as she rushed toward him. "Were you here to check on the house for Next Move or something? What a coincidence; Mr. Hunt, Heather's killer was just at the house. He lured me here and was going to kill me."

He laughed. "Let's not play games, Ms. Adams," he replied haughtily. "We both know what's going on here now, don't we?"

She raised an eyebrow. "What? What do you mean?" she asked in confusion. "I need help," she told him. "Heather's killer was at the house."

"I was not expecting you," he sighed as he eyed Tracy's frantic face. "But you'll do; Drew's body is upstairs, and now, *your* fingerprints are all over this house. I see you watered the plants and got a drink from the fridge? Wonderful."

Tracy stared at him as the realization of what was happening hit her like a train. "You," she murmured as Alex blinked at her. "You did it. You killed Heather...*and* Drew?"

He closed his eyes. "It wasn't an ideal situation," he began as he walked closer to her. "Heather's father did me wrong, Ms. Adams; he promised me complete control of the company upon his death, and then, he left his shares to Heather."

"But he was your best friend."

"Not in death," he laughed. "We built this company from scratch, but that didn't matter to him. He sold me out for his daughter. And then, even worse: I was stuck with her simple husband, who didn't know the first thing about business. What was I supposed to do, sit by and let him ruin my life's work?"

Her eyes widened. "So you killed them..."

"In cold blood," he smiled manically. "Again, not how I wanted things to go, but sometimes, these things happen."

He raised his arm, and she flinched. "You think I'm going to hit you?" he smirked as he scratched an itch on his back. "Ms. Adams, I don't need to hurt you; there is more than sufficient evidence to show you were here when Drew was murdered. And if they charge you for that, they'll certainly nail you for Heather's murder."

She felt her knees buckle, and she willed herself to stay upright. "You can't do this," she told him, hating that her voice was shaking. "I didn't kill them. You did it."

"I did," he admitted, shrugging his shoulders. "But no one will ever know it."

Tracy then heard a faint sound, one that she was sure only she would recognize: the vibration of her cell phone. She glanced down at the ground, remembering she had not hung up her phone call with Warren when Alex Hunt had walked in.

Alex followed her gaze and picked up her cell phone from where she had placed it on the ground. His smirk vanished when he realized the phone was on and a call was going through. "Oh, no..."

He turned on his heel and darted out of the house. Tracy followed along behind him. "Stop, Alex," she yelled, but before she could reach him, he was tackled by two police officers.

Warren stepped out of the shadows and glared at Alex. "That's what you get for messing with my girl," he snapped before turning to Tracy and gathering her in his arms.

23

Tracy didn't remember banks feeling so chilly; though she was dressed in a light blue pantsuit with a fashionable white scarf tied around her neck, she shivered as she waited in the lobby.

It had been a week since the scene on Marshall Street; Alex Hunt had been charged with two counts of first-degree murder for the deaths of Heather and Drew, and Tracy's name had finally been cleared. She could not believe how much trouble could take place in a small town, but as she had driven into the city, she grew sad thinking of leaving the small town.

She felt nervous as she waited to be called back for the job interview; Warren had seemed indifferent about whether or not she should attend, and she felt a bit out of place as she sat watching people trek across the marble floors.

Tracy took a sip of coffee and sighed, leaning back in the stiff leather chair as she waited.

"Tracy Adams?"

She turned to see Courtney Tucker, a banker she had occasionally worked with. "Courtney?"

Courtney smiled. She was a tall woman with dirty blonde hair and a perfect white smile. "I thought you moved to the burbs, stranger! What are you doing back in the city?"

Tracy grinned. She had always liked Courtney, and she was happy to see a familiar face. "I'm interviewing here," she told her. "Remember Isabelle? I think you two worked on a project a few years ago? Anyway, she works here, and I might, too!"

"Wonderful," Courtney beamed. "I hear the culture is great here; I'm actually running some documents up for a collaboration we are working on. I could put in a good word for you."

"That would be great," she told Courtney.

Courtney blinked. "So, back to the city, huh?" She asked curiously. "Had enough of small town life?"

Tracy shrugged. "I just don't know if I was cut out for a small town," she confessed. "I miss the lights and buzz of the city sometimes."

"That makes sense," her friend affirmed. "So, what were you doing in the suburbs? Banking?"

"Working at a flower shop," she shared. "I know-it was a huge pivot away from the finance industry, but I love the people, the slow pace, and the chance to be creative."

"Slow pace?"

Tracy nodded. "I work a few days a week, and when I am finished for the night, that's it. No working until two in the morning, no taking work home with me when it's over, and no frantic calls from my boss. It's pretty nice."

The smile vanished from Courtney's face. "That does sound nice," she replied dreamily. "I don't remember the last time I took a vacation; I work eighteen hours a day nearly eight months out of the year, and even during the quiet months, I am usually at the office until eight or nine at night."

"That's how it used to be for me," Tracy agreed. "Until I moved to Fern Grove."

Courtney pointed at her hand. "I see you picked up a little bling since you've been away," she winked. "Tell me about him. Have you set a date?"

"Warren is amazing," she gushed, running a hand through her hair and picturing her handsome fiancé. "He is a police officer, and he is kind, sweet, and a gentleman. He's totally different from everyone I dated here; he really has his head on straight."

"That must be nice to have a guy with his priorities in order," Courtney grumbled. "Everyone I meet in the city is either too concerned about their career or just wants a trophy wife to show off. It's impossible to meet a quality guy here."

Tracy smiled. "Come to Fern Grove and I could find someone for you," she teased. "Seriously, Courtney, there are so many cute, sweet guys there."

"I might have to make a trip over," Courtney agreed. "Are you sure you want to come back to a banking gig in the city, Tracy? Your life in your small town sounds pretty nice to me. A sweetheart of a fiancé, a job you love…what's the rush to come back to the city?"

Before Tracy could answer, Courtney's phone rang. She glanced down at it and frowned. "I'm late for my meeting," she informed Tracy as she bit her lip. "I have to run. It was so good catching up with you. Keep me posted on the job; if you end up back in the city, we'll have to meet for cocktails soon."

With that, she turned on her heel and floated away, her high heels clacking loudly on the marble floors.

Tracy took a long sip of her coffee. Courtney's words were weighing on her; she *did* have a great life in Fern Grove. Why did she feel like she needed to change things? She loved her job, her fiancé, and her close relationship with her aunt. Was she making the right decision?

Aunt Rose had been devastated to hear Tracy was still planning to interview for a job in the city. "You're really leaving? What about Warren? What about In Season?"

Tracy had explained that Warren could either commute or find a new job and that she had to follow her heart, that she wasn't sure if her heart was set on staying in Fern Grove.

"After two years, isn't this your home?" her aunt tearfully pleaded, but Tracy had not given her a response.

Tiffany was inconsolable. "How can you abandon us?" she moaned, her face dark. "We're a family, Tracy. You and Aunt Rose are the two people who mean the most to me in this entire world."

Tracy had felt a pang of guilt at Tiffany's words, but she knew she had to go through with the interview. If she didn't, she would always wonder what would have been, and she did not want to have any regrets.

"Tracy?"

Out of the corner of her eye she saw Andrew Meeks, a financial analyst she knew from her old job. "Andrew," she greeted him. "How are you?"

He strode over to her and smiled widely. "I'm headed upstairs to a meeting," he told her. "Good to see you; it's been a while."

She explained she had moved to Fern Grove and was back for an interview. "I hope you get the job," he told her. "I can't imagine how bored you must have been in your hometown; the city is where the action is, and the city is where people like us belong."

She raised an eyebrow. "There's action in Fern Grove," she said defensively. "My fiancé, Warren, and I have a lot of fun there; we go to the beach, and spend time with our friends, and we love going to the high school to watch the football games."

Andrew laughed. "That sounds just as fun as going to the hottest clubs and the sexiest bars," he joked, his sarcasm heavy. "Well, I have to run, but I hope you get the job, Tracy. Good luck to you. And welcome back to the city!"

She waved goodbye, feeling annoyed. Who was Andrew Meeks, someone she didn't even know that well, to talk down to her about living in Fern Grove? She sighed. Fern Grove wasn't the most cosmopolitan place in the world, but it was filled with good people and wholesome fun. She loved her little town, and she did not like that someone had put it down.

"Tracy? They are ready for you," a young male secretary came out and informed her. "Follow me."

Tracy followed him into a conference room where two interviewers were waiting for her. She did not recognize them, and they stood up and introduced themselves before shaking her hand.

"Myrna Small," the one on the left, a tall brunette with curly hair told her. "It's a pleasure."

"Amandeep Kaur," the one of the right greeted her, an olive-skinned woman in a gray suit.

"Please, have a seat."

She sat down, and the interview began.

"Isabelle told us a lot about you," Myrna smiled warmly. "We are so excited to have you here. What questions do you have for us about the position?"

"None at the moment," she told them truthfully. "But I will let you know at the end if any come up."

Myrna nodded. "Excellent."

"Tracy, tell us about your work experience since parting ways with your previous bank," Amandeep urged her.

She told them all about In Season, focusing specifically on

her management responsibilities and project management opportunities. She discussed the partnership with Next Move, telling them about how this deal had increased profits significantly for the shop.

"That's nice," Myrna said sweetly. "But I was hoping you would speak about your banking experience."

"Oh," Tracy stopped. "I'm so sorry."

Amandeep nodded. "No worries. Please, tell us about a time you solved a problem at work. We would love to hear about your problem-solving skills."

Tracy smiled. "We had an order that went awry," she began, not noticing the sour look on the interviewers faces. "It was a massive order, and the teenager we have working for us made a lot of mistakes. She said they wanted twelve baskets of roses when they needed twelve hundred. I ended up renting an RV, driving to Portland, collecting the additional roses, and arriving at the wedding on time. It was a stressful day, but by keeping a positive attitude and having an open mind, we managed to pull things off without a hitch."

Myrna wrinkled her nose. "Tracy, banking experiences, remember? Really, comparing a flower shop to an international chain of banks? That's quite bold, don't you think? I don't think I quite understand how the experiences connect…"

She cleared her throat. "Well, a flower shop is a business, just as a bank is," she declared, holding her head high and looking Myrna right in the eye. "It was a smaller scale operation, but I was able to gain skills and insights while flexing skills I learned during my career at the previous bank."

Amandeep raised an eyebrow. "Can you talk about the skills and insights you gained at the little flower shop?"

Tracy forced herself to smile politely. "I enhanced my client management skills," she told them. "I learned entirely new skill sets, including how to make things aesthetically pleasing. It's important to make things beautiful, and that is something I've learned along the way."

Myrna shot Amandeep a look. "I'm not quite sure making bouquets qualifies one for work at a bank..."

She scowled. "Please, let her speak," she urged her colleague.

"We don't have time to have our time wasted," Myrna muttered under her breath.

"Excuse me?" Amandeep frowned.

"Hey, it's all okay," Tracy told them. "Please, what's the next question?"

Amandeep turned to Tracy. "Please," she asked politely. "Please, Ms. Adams, can you tell us about a tangible skill or lesson you were able to learn from your past in banking? Your flower shop work sounds intriguing, truly. But we need to know that you know how to add value in a bank setting."

Tracy stood up. "Look," she began, feeling strong and brave as she placed her hands on her hips and looked both interviewers in the face. "You may not understand my experiences, but they are important. I have a graduate degree, years of experience in banking, and a resume that shows that. What it doesn't show is the smile a bride has on her face when the bouquet that was made for her wedding day arrives even more beautiful than she dreamed. What my resume does not show is the way a grandmother feels when her granddaughter bought the perfect basket of flowers to bring to her in the hospital. What my resume doesn't show is all the times I have had to be creative and think outside of the box to help people get the look or experience they wanted."

Myrna pursed her lips. "I think that's enough for today."

"Yes, it is," Tracy declared. "I have learned more about myself in that small town flower shop than I ever imagined. In Season makes me better, bolder, and brighter, and I think

I belong there. I'm sorry for wasting your time, but I must be going."

With that, Tracy picked up her leather briefcase and sauntered out of the room, swinging her hips and smiling as she stepped outside into the brisk winter air. She took a long, deep breath, and she knew that she was going home to Fern Grove, once and for all.

As Tracy left the office suite and took the elevator to the lobby, she had a huge smile on her face. She had had an epiphany of sorts in the interview; she knew where she belonged, and she knew where her heart had always been. She was ready to get home. Her feelings of restlessness quieted as she marched through the lobby.

"Wait!"

Tracy turned around to find Amandeep running after her. "Ms. Adams, wait."

She stopped and turned to face her. "Can I help you?"

"Please," she urged Tracy, shoving a set of papers toward her. "We want to offer you the position. I know Myrna gave you a hard time, but that was just part of our interview strategy. Good cop and bad cop, you know? We've looked over your resume, and from what you've told us, along with Isabelle's recommendation, we want to offer you the position."

Tracy smiled politely. "I'm sorry, but I don't think that's what I want."

Amandeep stared at her. "This is a highly coveted job," she informed her, still holding the papers. "You will be making more money than at your previous banking job, and there is so much potential to move up here. Please think about it, Ms. Adams."

Tracy shook her head. "I'm sorry for taking your time," she replied genuinely. "Truly, I am. I just don't think I belong in a bank anymore. It isn't the place for me."

"Are you sure? This is your last chance," Amandeep advised her. "There's no turning back if you walk out those doors."

Tracy shrugged. "Thank you for your time," she replied, turning on her heel and giving a little wave. "I know where I belong now."

Tracy walked to the parking garage with a huge grin on her face. She made it back to town in record time and drove over to Warren's house with sandwiches in hand to surprise him for lunch.

"Hey," he hugged her as she bounded into the house. "I thought you were going to be in the city most of the day."

"Plans change," she shrugged. "I don't want to leave Fern Grove. I want to make a life here. With you."

He grinned. "I hoped you would come to your senses."

They sat down to eat, and she filled him in on her outburst in the interview. "I wish I could have seen that," he groaned as she recounted how she stormed out of the room. "The way you called them out sounds so sexy, Babe."

"Warren," she squealed playfully, her heart soaring as she realized she had truly found her place in the world.

His smile faded. "I need to fill you in on some things that happened while you were out of town this morning," he told her, and she felt her heart begin to race.

"What's wrong?"

"It's about the Blackwood case."

She leaned back in her chair. "Did they find out anything else about Alex Hunt? I thought he was refusing to talk?"

"He finally confessed," Warren told her, his eyes wide. "His big-time lawyer must have told him that he would never make it in a jury trial. He confessed to everything in hopes of getting a nice plea deal."

She frowned. "What did he say?"

"Almost exactly what he said to you in that house,"

Warren explained. "Alex killed Heather out of greed and envy. He was furious when Mr. Hampton didn't give him the company outright."

She hung her head. "What a jerk."

"It's worse," he cautioned her. "He lured Heather to the Marshall house, and she had no concerns because he was like a second father to her. He killed her in cold blood, just as he said."

She wrinkled her nose. "What about Aunt Rose and the messages and the calls?"

"He confessed to all of it," he stated. "He made friends with Aunt Rose through Facebook and was able to set it up so that you were in the wrong place at the wrong time at the first house. After things started to fall apart when Drew Blackwood wasn't charged, he killed Drew, and his plan was to pin the murder on Aunt Rose and say you two had something to do with it."

She shook her head. "He really thought this thing out. So how did he drag Sean Barnes into it?"

"He faked an email to Sean that said a buyer wanted to see a house and would meet him there. He thought if things fell apart by blaming it all on Rose, he could throw Sean under the bus."

"He sounds like some sort of evil genius," she commented, shaking her head and reaching for her fiancé's hands. "It's a shame Mr. Hampton *didn't* leave Next Move to him; his daughter would still be alive, and with such a methodical mind, he could have taken the company to new heights."

Warren's eyebrows knitted together into a deep frown. "He's going to be locked up for a very long time," he informed her. "Anyway, enough about this mess. It's all over with and the important thing is that you are safe. Tell me, Tracy, are you sure you want to be in Fern Grove with me forever? You're sure this is what you really want? It made me nervous that you went to that interview; I thought maybe you were unhappy here and unhappy with me."

She reached over and took his face in her hands and planted a huge kiss on his lips. "My home is here, Warren. With you. Forever and always, until death do us part!"

He beamed. "It's gonna be a good life together, Miss Tracy," he winked as he leaned down and returned her kiss. "It's gonna be a good life!"

24

Later that afternoon, Tracy sashayed into In Season with a huge smile on her face.

"Hey, aren't you supposed to be in the city?" Tiffany asked as she came over to give her a hug.

"Nope," she winked. "City life is not for me, ladies."

Aunt Rose's eyes widened. "Wait, so does this mean..."

"I'm not taking a job in the city," she shared with them as Aunt Rose clapped her hands in excitement. "My life is here in Fern Grove."

Tiffany pulled them in for a group hug. "This is the best news," she cried.

"Yeah, it is," she agreed, squeezing her Aunt and Tiffany hard.

"We've had too much excitement around here," her aunt declared. "The only excitement I need in the future is thinking about your wedding. No more murders and no more witch hunts. Only love and happiness in this flower shop!"

Tracy nodded. "I agree."

Tiffany batted her eyelashes. "Do I get to bring a guest to

your wedding?"

Tracy tilted her head and looked at her. "Tiffany," she began. "I see no problem with hat but I think it might be too early in the process to give you a definitive answer."

Aunt Rose agreed. "She's right, Tiffany. It's a bit too early. Now, Tracy, I am curious... have you made any plans? Booked more vendors? The date is a few months off, but it's important to plan ahead."

"I know, I know," she laughed. "I was thinking about getting a cake from Sandy Bay. Have you two heard of that famous baker there? I've heard she's practically famous and can make a gorgeous wedding cake."

"My sister's hairdresser's uncle's niece got her wedding cake from there," Tiffany squealed. "I think that place is called Really Nice? Or Very Sugary? Something like that."

Aunt Rose's eyes sparkled. "We'll have to go dress shopping soon," she said dreamily. "I can picture you in a ballgown, or something with sparkles and a long train."

"Nope," Tracy chuckled. "I want a simple, clean wedding dress; we want a quiet wedding, nothing big or fancy."

Just then, the front door of the flower shop opened and Sean Barnes strolled in. He winked at Tracy. "What a pleasure seeing you in better circumstances," he greeted her. "Ladies, good evening."

"How can we help you?" Aunt Rose asked him. "Are you looking for a particular arrangement?"

He stared at Tracy. "I got my first multi-million dollar house to sell," he informed them. "And I need to make arrangements to have some staging done. I would love to fill the house with flowers. Do you ladies know anyone who could help me out?"

Tracy smiled in spite of herself. "Congratulations, Sean," she told him earnestly. "That's a huge accomplishment."

He wolfishly flashed his white smile at her. "I hope you

ladies can help me; I have a *huge* budget for flowers to stage the house, and I would love to give you the business."

Tracy nodded. "I think we can make something work," she assured him, her lips curling up into a smile. "What do you think, ladies?"

"YES!" Tiffany cried. "I'll be able to buy my car. And Rose, you could upgrade your cell phone. Think of how nice your Facebook photos would be with an even newer phone."

Rose giggled. "I think I'm done with social media for a while," she announced. "I think an old gal like me needs to just stick to the basics. I have a little surprise, girls. I hired a matchmaker to introduce me to some nice fellas. I am going to get out there and date again!"

Tracy's jaw dropped. "A matchmaker?"

Sean smiled. "I think it's a lovely idea," he cooed. "Your gorgeous sister deserves to meet someone nice."

"She's my aunt," Tracy told him, and he smiled.

"Your aunt? Wow. Those are some good genes."

Aunt Rose smiled at the compliment. "That's too kind of you," she told him. "I think this new partnership is off to a great start."

Around three in the afternoon, the three ladies walked over to Grind it Out for a quick break. Tiffany grabbed a corner booth in the back, and Tracy and Rose made their way to the line to place their order.

As they waited, Tracy felt a tap on her shoulder. She turned around and frowned when she found Burt Brock, the reporter, standing behind her with a weak smile on his face.

"Fueling up?" he asked kindly.

"Yes," she replied curtly, remembering how he had twisted her words on the news.

"Hey," he said in a hushed tone. "I just wanted to apologize to you, Tracy. I feel bad that our news team ambushed you in front of the flower shop. That wasn't right."

She stared at him. "I didn't have anything to do with Heather's death," she told him. "And I think you knew that didn't you?"

He shrugged. "I was in a bit of a pickle, you see," he murmured. "I was tipped off about you by someone very influential."

"Tipped off? What do you mean?"

He ran a hand through his hair. "Alex Hunt contacted me," he sighed, looking down at his shiny leather shoes. "He sent over a copy of the police report from when you were taken in. I didn't understand *why* he sent it over or how he got the report, but with that kind of information, I had to act quickly before another news outlet got hold of it."

Her eyes widened. "Alex Hunt sent you the police report?"

"He did," Burt confirmed. "I know he's been involved in a lot of charity work with the station and is good friends with the chief. All I know is he wanted to throw us off and set you up."

She crossed her arms over her chest. "I can't believe it."

"Journalism can get ugly," he informed her, his smile vanishing. "Especially when we get the facts wrong. I'm sorry about that, too."

She nodded. "Thank you. I hope you think of me the next time you want to run out and stick a microphone in someone's face. Everyone has feelings, and I hope you don't forget that."

He agreed. "You're right. I won't, Tracy. I won't forget."

She smiled. "I'm glad to hear it."

They said goodbye, and Aunt Rose turned to her. "What was that all about?" She asked as she balanced her latte and Tiffany's cappuccino in her hands.

"He apologized for ambushing me," Tracy explained, taking her matcha smoothie off of the counter and following her aunt back to their table. "I accepted his apology, but I reminded him he needs to think about the feelings of the people he reports on."

"That was a good idea," her aunt praised. "I think we *all* need that reminder sometimes."

They returned to their table and sat down. Tiffany was grinning as Rose handed her the cappuccino.

"What are you smiling about?" Tracy asked the teenager.

"I decided which car I want," she told them, pulling out her phone and showing them a photo of a red Honda civic. "I think I'll look so cute in this."

Rose studied the picture. "Red, honey? Are you sure? Aren't there statistics about the police pulling over red cars more often than they pull over any other color?"

Tiffany rolled her eyes. "That can't be true."

Tracy laughed. "How about I ask Warren? He can settle this matter."

"Deal."

She pulled out her cell phone and texted a message to her fiancé. He did not respond right away, and she put her phone back in her pocket.

Tracy looked around the table and felt her heart warm as her aunt smiled back and Tiffany drank her coffee. She glanced down as her engagement ring caught the light and started sparkling, and she felt so much gratitude for everything going on in her life. She loved her aunt, adored her friends, found her job fulfilling, and was going to marry the love of her life in just a few short months. She could not believe how blessed she was.

"Why are you smiling like that?" Her aunt asked. "What is that look on your face, Tracy?"

"Oh, nothing," she told them. "I'm just *happy*. And it feels really, really good."

The End

AFTERWORD

Thank you for reading Missing Heather and Bad Weather! I really hope you enjoyed reading it as much as I had writing it!

If you have a minute, please consider leaving a review on Amazon or the retailer where you got it.

Many thanks in advance for your support!

CARNATIONS AND DEADLY FIXATIONS

CHAPTER 1 SNEEK PEEK

ABOUT CARNATIONS AND DEADLY FIXATIONS

Released: August, 2019
Series: Book 1 – Fern Grove Cozy Mystery Series

Tracy Adam had three things going for her in her just-above-average boring life namely:

1. A good job
2. A good job… that she liked
3. A good job that she liked… and paid VERY well

When she lost her job and had to move back to the small town where she grew up, it seemed like her life had lost all purpose. Helping out at her aunt's floundering floral shop seemed like the perfect distraction before she decided what to do next.

When her aunt's competition, a nasty and egotistical know-it-all is found dead, the rumor mill in Fern Grove goes into overdrive. With an important piece of evidence linking Tracy to the scene of the crime, she becomes a person of interest in the murder investigation. This leaves her feeling vulnerable and confused.

Moving back to Fern Grove was meant to be start of a new life but this murder mystery is fast ending what has hardly begun. Will she retain her wits and piece the clues that will lead her to the killer?

CHAPTER 1 SNEAK PEEK

Tracy Adams popped her work apron over her head as she made her way out of the back of In Season, the small, but established flower shop her aunt, Rose Bishop had founded with her husband, Frank, many years ago.

In the few moments of peace and quiet that she knew would be short-lived once her aunt arrived, Tracy sipped at her coffee and her mind wandered. Tracy would never have imagined that her life would have taken the sharp detour it had.

At thirty-eight, and with the trajectory that her once burgeoning professional life had been on, helping run a somewhat floundering florist shop had sure not been on her menu. She had landed her dream job right out of The University of Portland, doing event-planning for CMB Capital, an up and coming bank in Portland, Oregon. Her future looked as bright as could be imagined until some questionable speculations by the senior management team put the high flying financial new comer in jeopardy.

Once decisions had been made, it was like this rolling tide

that everyone could see coming, but were unable to stem. She observed as colleagues and friends at CMB were told their positions had been deemed "redundant". Tracy despised all forms of euphemistic language, but this term especially raised her ire; like calling the blow that you were about to be laid off could be softened by this word. She held her breath and prayed she would survive the cutbacks, but in her heart, she knew her position as an event planner was most likely not an essential role for CMB's survival.

The days went by and Tracy actually began to believe she had somehow been spared. But then one morning her boss, William Atherton, the man who had recruited her out of her undergraduate program, came with the bad news she had been dreading. Though he promised she would be one of the last of the furloughed staff to be dismissed, due to her great work since coming onboard and her undying loyalty to CMB, it was just empty words. She was sure Atherton had been sincere in his pronouncement to her, as she could see on his face when her dismissal came down, that the decision had most likely come from above him.

So here she was, back in her small hometown of Fern Grove once more, looking out the window at *In Season*, the family business she had known as a child. After losing her job at CMB, it had been a struggle, for Tracy as well as a lot of others, to recover and acquire new professional positions. She was starting to get a little frantic as to what she would do and how she was going to pay her bills when her Aunt Rose inquired as to whether she would be interested in coming to the florist shop and helping her out. Rose had become like a mother-figure to Tracy ever since her mother, Madeline, Rose's sister, had died suddenly in a traffic accident when Tracy was just fifteen. Rose and her husband had founded and grown In Season from scratch and it had, over time, become very popular in Fern Grove. Once a successful businesswoman in Fern Grove, the death of Frank was the catalyst that led to Rose neglecting the business. That, plus having her own kids move out of Fern Grove and then away from Oregon as well, had dampened her drive and though still respected in town, Rose was just feeling fatigued and mowed down by the circumstances in her life.

During a call with her aunt one day, Tracy had innocently inquired as to how things were going at In Season, as she knew Rose was struggling with all the downturns she had encountered as of late. She could hear the sadness in her voice and though she was concerned, she had never ever considered helping out until Rose just came out with it.

"I don't know, Tracy..." Rose said with a heavy sigh, "some days I just do not know..."

"Aunt Rose?" Tracy asked as her aunt's voice just trailed off without any seeming direction.

"It's just not the same without Frank anymore. Flowers are not moving the way they used to, and some days it just seems too overwhelming, you know?"

"Maybe time for some changes?"

"Maybe...maybe...you still looking for a job?"

"You know I am, Aunt Rose."

"You had a really high-flying position over at CMB before they nearly went under doing corporate events, seminars and job fairs...things like that, right?"

"Yes..."

"Maybe with that experience, you could join me and help me turn this place around."

Tracy paused as she had not been expecting this. However, there was a part of her that was excited at the prospect of remolding *In Season* back into what it had once been...maybe even better! She smiled over the phone, welcoming the challenge to bring some 'big business' concepts and strategies she had learned to a small business.

Without any more hesitation, her brain was already bubbling with innovative strategies and modern plans for action. Her only real hurdle, she knew, was going to be her aunt.

She knew Rose was still stuck in the mind-set she and Frank had instituted when they had begun when Tracy was just a little girl. Times were changing all around, even in Fern Grove, and the way people were looking at and purchasing flowers was evolving as well. But Rose seemed resistant to change with the times. Part of it was her age, Tracy knew, and she was sure Rose might be a bit intimidated by how technology was impinging on everything these days—something that was likely to be as foreign to her aunt as waking up one day and discovering she now had three heads. Tracy was sure she could overcome it, just as she had other similar instances in her life.

Having lost her husband and then having her kids move far away, Tracy knew, was part of her aunt's inertia as well. It had taken the fire out of her belly after she had been so successful. And all of this together was contributing to the downturn in revenue at In Season. The last time Tracy had been to the shop she was struck by just how frumpy and old-fashioned the interior appeared in relation to the new shops that had opened around town. Tracy readily agreed to help her out; somewhat out of an obligation to her aunt who had caught her when she was collapsing after her mother's demise, but also it was just her nature to want to help out when she was asked. However, the one stipulation was that Rose allow Tracy to institute some serious changes to the shop—ones that would bring In Season into the 21st century. Rose reluctantly conceded, but in the tone of her voice, Tracy could envision this being a struggle.

* * *

In just another minute, Rose came in and gave Tracy a confused look as she closed the door of the shop behind her.

"What's with the banner outside?"

Tracy had arrived early to hang the *"Temporarily Closed While We Prepare for the Grand Opening of the New In Season"* sign.

"Remember our agreement, Aunt Rose?"

"OK...OK.... but I cannot stay closed too long or we will never recover lost customers."

"Fair enough. You are going to have to change with the times, Aunt Rose. Like it or not. I know you love to talk about the good old days, and how you and Uncle Frank used to do things. But if you want to keep this place open and make it a going enterprise again, we need to try some new approaches."

Rose nodded, but Tracy could see she was not real sure. Tracy motioned to Rose to follow her to the back where she had sketched out a strategy. Rose looked at the designs and notes and Tracy could tell this was going to be a harder sell than she had imagined.

"My idea is to select a popular flower each few months and make that the centerpiece showcase around which everything else revolves. To begin with, I chose the carnation."

"Carnations? Really?" Rose asked. "Pretty common flower in my opinion."

"Perhaps, but popular with the world nonetheless. Did you know, for example, that the carnation dates back over 2000 years? They are rich in symbolism and mythology as well."

Rose did not reply.

"And each color is attached to an emotion: white for love and good luck, while red is seen for admiration and deeper love and affection while purple colors imply vulnerability or fickleness. Most impactful are the pink colors, though. This variety originates from the story that they first appeared from the Virgin Mary's tears which became symbolic for a mother's undying love."

"And that helps us, how?"

"You need to really market your products, Aunt Rose. They are not just flowers. I am telling you, from my experience at CMB, that an elaborate story behind something simple—or common as you put it about the carnation—makes the ordinary seem extraordinary."

"I guess...why did you leave that fancy-schmancy job anyway?"

"Aunt Rose, can you please not bring that up. I am here to help you out until I can figure out what is next for me."

"Sure...sorry. I did not mean to bring that up again."

Tracy then went back to her designs to explain in more detail to Rose just how this was going to work and what other flowers she might consider down the road as different focal points to avoid having one type get stale and predictable.

"Think change and innovation and allure, Aunt Rose...."

Just then there was a sharp knock at the front door. They both looked up suddenly wondering who this could be as the closed sign with the announcement of a relaunch was clearly visible. Tracy went to check and felt her spirits sink as she saw who had come calling. Before opening the door and greeting the visitor, Tracy turned to her aunt.

"Hate to ruin your day, Aunt Rose, but it would appear your competition has arrived. I am guessing the signage was too much of a curiosity factor to ward her off."

Rose looked to the closed door, and like Tracy, had no idea the day could get any worse. Never say never she mumbled to herself...

Carnations and Deadly Fixations

FERN GROVE COZY MYSTERY

ABBY REEDE

ALSO BY ABBY REEDE

The Fern Grove Cozy Mystery Series

Printed in Great Britain
by Amazon

69611664R00102